OPERATION FENLAND

BY
WILLIAM MEIKLE

SEVERED**PRESS**

OPERATION FENLAND

Copyright © 2025 by William Meikle

WWW.SEVEREDPRESS.COM

ISBN: 978-1-923165-98-4

- DUFFIELD -

Captain Banks did not look happy and that in itself was more than enough to make Duffield's own worries all the more apparent. Being called in from home with a wake-up call at five in the morning was never going to be a good sign, and the young lieutenant had fretted all the way down the road to Lossiemouth. The bacon roll he'd grabbed from the van on the north side of the Kessock Bridge lay in his stomach like a brick, and his concern must have shown in his face, for the captain looked up and smiled thinly as the younger man entered his C.O.'s office.

The captain already looked well settled in his new role; his name was on the office door, he'd had an old tatty chair replaced by a new thing of chrome and leather that looked like it cost what Duffield made in a year, and he had the windows open, letting the sea air and the sound of angry crows in from the trees surrounding the base.

"Why the long face, lad? Dinna fash yerself," Banks said from behind the desk. "It's no' you that's got ma knickers twisted. You're not in trouble. No' this time anyway. I've had orders, and I never take too kindly to being shat on from any height, never mind one as high as this. Have a seat and we'll both see if we can make any sense of it."

1

He brandished a sheaf of papers as Duffield took the rather less salubrious seat opposite.

"They got me out of my scratcher for this at two o'clock this morning, so somebody's definitely got a bee up his arse about it somewhere."

Duffield waited. It was obvious the captain needed to vent at somebody. Better for the squad if Duffield took the brunt of it now rather than them having to take it later. Besides, he knew Banks to be a good officer; it would blow over soon enough once duty kicked in to override annoyance. He just hoped he didn't have to wait too long.

The captain was still waving the papers around.

"Fucking pencil pushers. What do they ken about anything? Fuck all, that's what. They've asked me to send a team to Norfolk. The S-Squad in particular. Fucking Norfolk? What kind of beastie are they expecting down there apart from some inbred bumpkins? And there's no sign, no hint as to why they want us or why they're in so much of a fucking hurry. 'Requested from the highest levels of Government' it says. We all ken what that means. There's shite that needs shovelling and as usual we're the ones who are going to be hip deep in it."

Duffield chanced a remark in the hope of moving the conversation along.

"Young Mac has contacts in the Ministry, through his auld man, doesn't he?" Duffield asked. "Maybe he could help to clear things up?"

Banks shook his head. He was still angry but it seemed to be dissipating and at least he'd stopped waving the papers around. He sighed deeply, took out a cigarette case and offered a smoke. Duffield declined with a wave of the hand; too early in the morning to be chugging smoke down on top of a dodgy burger. Banks lit up before replying.

"I tried Mac's auld man and got fucking nowhere except for getting a bollocking for waking him up on a day off," Banks replied, and banged his palm angrily against his stiff leg as if it offended him. "And there's this…"

He took an envelope from his desk drawer and tossed it across the desk. It bore an official looking stamped wax seal, and had written on the front 'Only to be opened by the senior officer once on site.'

"I cannae even open it to tell you what's in it. But I suspect it's more Whitehall fucking fuckery. The whole thing reeks of fucking wee green men and X-Files black ops shite to me," Banks said, 'and I've never had much time for either."

He sighed loudly again and took a deep drag of his smoke before passing the sheaf of papers over to put in a wee pile beside the envelope.

"You'll need to read this, but I can tell you now it's mostly shite… we can only hope there's something in the envelope with more concrete details on what you're heading into. I'd been hoping you'd get more time with the men before sending you on a live case but it looks like fate has pished in our mouths again. Get the squad together, lad, you're heading for the fens. And suit up in wet weather gear. The forecast is for rain… a fuckload of it."

The only good thing about the situation was that the squad members were already on base so he didn't have to spend time in rounding them up. He called them together for a meeting in the mess and put a pot of coffee on to brew.

Private MacIntosh, aka Mac, arrived first, a rather quiet young lad who didn't smile much but was grateful for a mug of coffee. His record was one of service punctuated by bouts of temper in the early stages of his career, one of which had almost led to him being kicked out the service entirely. As Duffield mentioned to the captain earlier, Mac's father held a position in the M.O.D. that gave him enough clout to keep the lad in a job. How far that nepotism might extend, and how it might affect the lad's performance, was something Duffield had yet to figure out, although he had no complaints on that front in their job down the cave in Austria. It was something only time would tell, if they were given it.

Corporal Wilkins, aka Wilko, came in next, all smiles and good cheer. Duffield knew that masked a chequered history of injury and hardship on previous missions, one in particular where he had almost lost the use of his legs and had suffered through a long, painful period of recuperation before working his way back onto the team. But the lad's record spoke for itself, being one of courage and steadfastness in the face of some pretty weird shit.

The fact he was gay was neither here nor there, although Sergeant Wiggins had made a point of telling Duffield that the lad's smile was '... wasted on him. It would get him into any lassie's knickers in minutes if he was that way inclined.'

The aforementioned sergeant was last to arrive. Wiggins, aka Wiggo, was the longest standing member of the team, having been on board since the early mission to Antarctica and the Nazi UFO base and having worked his way up from private over the course of the years in between. He was shorter by a few inches than the others, older too, with grey flecks starting to show at his temples. He walked with that distinctive swagger common to a certain era of Glaswegian lads, held himself well and was stocky with it. His reputation was as a well-known 'mouthy wee git', a first class soldier, and a stout friend to his friends, although rumour had it there weren't many of those. He'd seen numerous squad members come and go, some retired, some promoted, too many others KIA, but was now, for the first time, in a situation of having a new man in charge of 'his' squad. Duffield had got this post over Wiggo's head, and the young lieutenant still wasn't sure of their relationship, despite them having come through the thing in Austria side by side. Again, it was something that only time would tell. This being Duffield's first taste of field command meant there was a lot he was trusting to his judgement. He could only hope it was sound.

There were the usual grumbles as they gathered around the coffee pot, especially from Wiggo who'd got rousted from his bed while nursing a hangover. The sergeant was as equally enamoured of the situation as Banks had been earlier.

"Fucking Norfolk? There's nowt there but wet grass, marshland and crap fitba teams. Why the fuck would they send us there?"

At least getting the briefing went quietly, and getting the squad prepped for the weather, and weapons, such as they'd be allowed on home soil, stowed went smooth and by the numbers. But once they were boarded on the plane to take them south, more coffee in hand, Wiggo was making his feelings known to Wilkins and Mac.

Duffield still wasn't sure whether to give him rein or whether he should be tightening the leash.

Wiggo showed no signs of backing off.

"Fucking Norfolk," he said again, shaking his head. He looked over at Duffield and grinned. "I blame the new boss."

"Aye?" Duffield said, "Well, I blame sergeants who run their mouths and their arses at the same time. Are you going to keep this shite up the whole job?"

Corporal Wilkins laughed loudly.

"You expect him to break the habits of a lifetime, boss? He's only happy when he's moaning. He's going to love the fucking rain."

That earned Wilkins a cuff around the ear from Wiggo, and an accompanying laugh from Duffield.

"Good to see we've started as we mean to go on. Now keep the noise down," he said. "We're going in blind. May as well be quiet at the same time."

Mac piped up.

"Do you not have a clue as to what we're facing?"

"Not a Scooby," Duffield replied. "And Captain Banks even asked your auld man."

"He must have been desperate," Mac replied, and went quiet, turning his head away.

Sore subject.

Duffield didn't push it; now wasn't the time to be opening old wounds.

The pilot asked them to take their seats and prepare for take-off. Duffield moved two rows down the empty plane to get a double seat to himself.

"You going to open yon envelope?" Wiggo said, coming up at his back.

"Orders are not to, until we're on site."

"Aye? So are you going to open it?"

Duffield laughed.

"Just sit down, Sarge, and you'll find out in good time."

Wiggo smiled and retreated.

"You're gonna open it. I bet you a fiver on it."

Truth told, it was a fiver Duffield was going to lose because his Sarge had seen through him so easily, so early in their new relationship. Duffield had been proud as punch when Banks asked him to take over the squad, but walking in on an already established squad was never going to be as smooth as he'd have liked, and now Wiggo was clearly intent on pushing the barriers to see how much leeway he was going to be allowed.

"Not a fucking lot if I get my way," Duffield muttered under his breath.

He read the loose sheaf of papers that Banks had handed him first but he'd already gone over that at the briefing; it was a simple statement of their orders, to head for Norfolk and await further instructions. That done, he gave in to the inevitable, took out the envelope and slit it open with a fingernail. There were three pages of a handwritten letter, and a thick wad of what looked like photocopied material. He picked the letter first.

He immediately recognised the name on the letterhead of the first page, but that only brought more confusion, for he could not fathom what it might imply.

It began, Dear Joe, so whoever wrote it knew in advance of his circumstances, which was in itself supposedly a secret. His confusion only grew as he read.

I'm probably the last person in the world you ever expected to hear from. And I'm sorry to have to drag you into this. I can only say that every word that follows is true. After that mess in London I know you to be a level-headed chap, but I also know the kind of things your new squad gets involved with. I'm afraid this may be a tad too esoteric, even for you and your men, but you're the only ones who might believe me without thinking it merely the delusions of a rambling old man long past his best.

There's some detail attached to this letter that you will need to read as soon as you can, but first I have a story you must hear. Trust me, this is all pertinent.

To begin at the beginning, I have to take you back to the Fifties. I was barely out of my teens, in pursuit of a girl. I was recently bereft of both parents, with a stipend large enough to see me through my degree, and an inheritance waiting for me when I came of age at twenty-one. I had mourned Mater and Pater sorely, but by the time the first term of the new University year came round I was ready to throw myself both into study and into a more sociable set of circumstances.

I was studying classics, but had already branched out in my own time into more esoteric studies, spending many hours in the Bodleian on ancient musty alchemical texts and grimoires, for even then my mind was taken by the mystic. That particular Christmas I went to the college ball in great anticipation, for I had heard that invites had been sent to several ladies' colleges and some new faces were to be expected.

And that is where I met Eleanor. She and I found ourselves partnered for an eightsome reel and by the end of the thing I had looked into her eyes and been immediately smitten. I was completely besotted and would have done anything for her. So when she came to me with a problem some days later I was only too happy to come to her aid.

Eleanor was from a Catholic Church background, her father being a priest in a small chapel in a rural town, and he was having a problem of a spiritual nature that was clearly of some delicacy and that he seemed loath to discuss with the family. Eleanor asked if I would be so kind as to have a word with her father and I said I would do it, for her. Two days later I was invited to her family house in the Norfolk Broads, on the edge of the village of Titmarsh.

She was my first love, and I was like a new puppy in her presence. I was starting to think my feelings were reciprocated, and this invitation to meet her parents had me hoping it was another step in cementing our future together.

Fate had other ideas in mind for me.

Titmarsh is a remarkably well preserved English village sitting in one of the few high spots surrounded by an ancient expanse of fenland. Back then it was well off the beaten track and I took several wrong turns on narrow country roads before coming across it almost by accident. But despite its remoteness, there proved to be a warm welcome waiting for me.

Eleanor's family home was a most charming thatched vicarage cottage of some great age, set in a secluded lane behind the old chapel which to my untrained eye looked decidedly Norman in aspect, if not even older. Her parents were most kind to me, making sure that I was going to be comfortable and want for nothing during my stay. We had a fine but simple supper, the conversation mainly revolving around their family matters and how proud they were of their girl.

After supper I took the opportunity of asking her father if he would be so kind as to show me his chapel, professing that I had a love for, and long interest in, historical buildings of a religious nature. This wasn't an attempt to ingratiate myself, for I was indeed genuinely interested in the history of the place. The older man led me along a shadowy lane through an ancient graveyard.

"There are stones here going back to the Saxon age," he said. "The chapel's foundations are also of that period, and in the crypt there is evidence that the Romans once worshiped Mithras on this very spot."

He pointed out a large monolith that dominated the center of the churchyard.

"And that old stone there tells me that the ground was sacred to somebody even before that. We are walking where many feet have trod to find their god, young man. Can you feel it?"

I could certainly feel the weight of history, and the chapel itself only served to heighten the sense of antiquity, being a squat, simple building with a turret rather than a steeple and retaining the old thatched roof rather than more modern slates.

"There is a tale that many of the faith took sanctuary here during Henry's purges," the older man said as he showed me inside. "Although it wouldn't have fitted very many of them."

He lit an oil lamp from beside the door and led me into what was little more than a box room some twelve feet by eight with four pews and an ancient pulpit and font before a clearly even more ancient altar. I saw that the altar itself was a rough hewn block of stone similar in composition to the menhir we'd passed in the graveyard, and it looked to be covered in crude carvings. I moved forward intending to take a closer look, but Edward seemed reluctant to approach, and I could see little without the benefit of the lamp.

The older man seemed suddenly rather squirrely, and was peering around as if searching for something in the shadows. A dog howled somewhere in the distance and he started, setting the lamp swinging and the shadows capering in the chapel's corners.

"It was just a dog," I said.

"You heard it too?" he asked, and I heard a tremor in his voice. It sounded like fear.

"Of course," I replied.

He lifted the lamp and looked me in the face then, as if he had come to a decision, led me back out into the graveyard.

"There is something I must show you, lad," he said. "If you heard, then perhaps you can also see."

He would not explain that remark, and scuttled off, taking the lamp with him and forcing me to follow sharply to keep up.

He led me out of the chapel and, not down the path, but down a slope between the stones through the graveyard, to the far end away from the house where the churchyard was bounded by an *old dry-stone dyke and a view looking out over a farmer's field to a wooded copse beyond. It was still twilight, and a clear night, so I had a clear view, but saw nothing untoward...at first.*

"There," he said, pointing to the copse. "Right at the edge of the field. You see it, don't you?"

At first all I saw was shadow under the tree branches. Then it moved and I did indeed see it. It was a dog, a great, shaggy, black beast of a thing the size of a pony, and when it looked my way its eyes were red fire, blazing suddenly bright in the gathering gloom. It lifted its head and howled, and my blood ran cold.

"What in blazes is that?" I asked.

"It is my doom,' Edward said baldly, and wandered off into the graveyard.

I found him sitting on a bench under an ancient yew filling a pipe. I lit up a smoke and sat down beside him. At first he seemed content to remain silent, but then he started to speak.

"It started coming two months ago now. At first it was just a distant howl in the night. Then a few weeks back, I'd see it loping in the fields in the distance, circling the chapel. These past few nights it has been in the copse above Old Tom's Tit. Now it is almost on the edge of the field. It comes closer. And when it is close enough, it will come to take me with it, and I shall have no choice but to go."

All of the above is preamble to the man's death shortly thereafter, which I am afraid occurred in my absence. You'll find supporting material accompanying my tale in the accompanying papers, but if you believe nothing else, believe this of me. The dog is real, and has been all along. I saw it, as clear as I saw you in London. You can ask Eleanor Wilkes herself at the vicarage when you arrive on site. She, like me, is old now, but I have it on good authority that her mind is yet sound. She will tell you.

The hound is very real.

And it is back.

Yours in good faith,

Your old friend George.

Duffield had met George a few years back, in London. The squad had seen off a big blobby bastard that had taken occupation in the Tube system, and after the job was done, Duffield had been sent in as leader of a team to clean shit up and keep a lid on the story. George, for reasons Duffield had never quite been able to fathom, had been his liaison to Whitehall. He had also proved, despite his age, to be quite the man for the ale, and they'd had several happy nights ensconced in old London pubs, but they'd hardly been what could be called friends, and it was definitely a surprise to hear from him again under such circumstances.

Duffield turned the three pages over, expecting more but there was nothing else, no further explanation. He turned to the photocopies. One paragraph immediately caught his eye, taken from an abstract of a paper called 'Apparitions of Black Dogs.'

Black dogs are often encountered near water, e.g. the sea, ponds, and bridges over streams or rivers (Bord & Bord, 1985). However, Bord & Bord (1985) also note that "there are very few places in Britain where one is very far away from water (except in times of drought!)". Bord and Bord (1985) theorised that black dogs might patrol ley lines and appear at various ley points such as churchyards, prehistoric remains and ancient trackways.

The rest of the photocopied pages were of little help, being mostly items copied from old books or faded newspaper clippings, and telling lurid tales of a giant hound terrorising a remote village, a smattering of stories from legend of harbingers of death, and, in several places, mention of Black Shuck, demon hound.

- HARRY -

Harry Greenfield had never seen so much rain, and that was quite an admission coming from a man of the fens. It had started yesterday, just after lunch, and steadily strengthened over the intervening time until it was now a roaring gale accompanied by what felt like a horizontal wall of water. And the forecast was that it was going to get worse before it got better.

Last night he'd determined that it was just another storm, that he would ride it out like he had ridden many another. Then he saw the weather forecast when he got out of bed, saw the great swirling thing that was about to fall on East Anglia, and knew this was going to be no ordinary drop of rain. As a lad Harry had sat by his granddad while the old man spoke with awe of the Great Storm of '53 and the damage it had wrought to the fens; the weatherman this morning had said this one might be worse than that.

Harry's first thought was for the safety of his animals. He'd been out in the gathering storm all morning, retrieving his flock from all quarters of his land to fetch them inside. His ram, Old Tom, a belligerent bugger at even the best of times, had ideas of his own, and had led Harry a merry dance through bog and coppice before finally deigning to lead the stragglers home to the barn, but by the time Harry had them all safely squared away inside he was like his land; thoroughly soaked and holding just about as much water as he was capable of carrying.

Once back in the warmth of the farmhouse, a change into dry clothes helped his mood, as did the knowledge that the sheep were all now safe from rising water. But he found himself, as he had many times before, rattling around in a house that felt too empty; it had been that way since his mother passed, two years before. Before she went she had made Harry promise to get a woman, settle down; easy words for her, a far harder job for Harry, who was more closely wed to the booze than he'd ever be to any woman.

The mere thought of a drink was, as usual, enough for him to entertain the idea of a lunchtime pint; it would mean going back out into the elements and another soaking, but that was a small price to pay for a few well-earned beers. He wrapped himself up in his waterproof, checked that the barn was firmly closed, and set off cross country.

The walk from his farmhouse to the village soon had him worried again. Despite the waterproofs the rain lashed against his oilskin jacket and ran off the brim of his hat down beneath his clothes at the neck, but he scarcely noticed the discomfort; all his attention was on the river. The Orin was as high as he'd ever seen it, and already a good foot up on earlier that morning, a brown spate tugging at rapidly eroding banks and slopping over into his fields in several places. At least the footpath was five feet higher still, but if the rain kept up even that was going to be underwater, and sooner rather than later.

Only the thought of a pie and a pint kept him from turning for home and locking himself in against the weather. There was a small crowd gathered in the playing fields, anxiously patrolling the river bank. Harry saw Jenny, the local police officer, and gave her a wave. She shouted something back but it was lost in the wind, and Harry was by now more intent on getting inside out of the rain than he was in walking over for a chat. He gave her a wave back that he hoped indicated that he'd speak to her later, and turned off onto the road up into the village.

When he walked into the bar his heart sank.

Old Bob Brown was holding forth from the corner seat and Harry immediately regretted the decision to leave the quiet comfort of home, for quiet was something Bob could never be accused of being.

Maybe I should have stopped for a chat with Jenny. Even in the rain it would have been preferable to this shite.

"She's tidal, see," the old man said in his customary bellow that could not be ignored in any corner of the bar. "And if the wind changes at high tide all that water's going to have nowhere to go. The fields will be the least of our problems. Just you wait and see."

"Yes, Bob, we heard you the first time," Dave, the barman said wearily. "And the second. Give it a rest will you. You're scaring my customers."

The only other customers were a couple that Harry recognised but didn't know, recent incomers who had bought a house in the village but were only around at weekends and bank holidays. But Dave had been right on one thing at least, the couple were gazing out at the rain, and they did indeed look worried.

Dave looked up, saw Harry, and immediately moved along the bar to pour him a pint.

"You look like you need this."

Harry took to the pint like a drowning man after a lifejacket and got three gulps down before replying.

"Been out in this shit all morning, rounding up the bastard sheep. Old Tom was being a right obstinate sod, as usual."

"Did you get them all in?" the barman asked.

"Eventually. As I said, Old Tom took a strop and had me chasing him around up the top field, but even he saw sense in the face of this crap. Have you ever seen anything like it?"

"I have," old Bob piped up. He was rarely quiet for long, and this proved to be no different. "Or at least my old man did. Back in '53. He said it was the wrath of God, biblical stuff. He said..."

"I remember your faither well," Dave replied. "And everybody remembers what he was like. It was getting him to shut the fuck up that was the problem. One you seem to have inherited, Bob. Now be a good lad and keep schtum, or I'll cut off your ale."

Bob was about to reply, but one look from Dave put an end to it... for now.

Dave kept his voice low, making it obvious that Bob was not included in the conversation as he addressed Harry.

"How's it looking out there? Will the banks hold?"

"Best guess? Fifty-fifty," Harry replied. "At least the village is on the higher ground, but it's the lower bridge I'd be worried about. If we do get a flood, that's the only way in or out, and it's not in a great state to start with."

"That's what Jenny said. She's away to have a gander. Should be back soon."

"I saw her, down by the playing fields."

"Yep. They're worried about that stretch too. She took a couple of the Town Council lads down with her to see if anything needs doing. What with that, and the flap at the vicarage, she's been run off her feet." Dave said.

"Vicarage? Something going on there? I hadn't heard."

"We'll all be hearing soon enough," Bob bellowed from the corner. "He's coming. He comes with the rain. He always comes with the rain. Everybody knows that."

"Bob, if you don't shut the fuck up, right fucking now, I swear..."

Dave didn't need to say any more. Bob fell quiet again as the barman turned to Harry.

"It's Eleanor, the old lady. She's got some bee in her bonnet. Says she's being menaced... hunted is what she says."

"Hunted? Who by?"

"Not who, what. She says it's a big black dog."

"Not that fucking Black Shuck story again?"

Dave nodded.

"That fucking Black Shuck story again. She thinks it got her old faither all those years ago, and now it's back for her."

"Let me guess. There's no sign there's any kind of dog on the prowl at all? And Jenny's getting grief from the old lady?"

"Right. And it seems that there's plenty of grief to be going around."

"And more to come," Bob bellowed from the corner seat. "Just you wait and see."

Harry limited himself to just the pie and two pints; the allure of more was always large in his mind but he'd toughened himself against that call after his mother died, trying to make an effort in her memory, and today wasn't a day for any internal slippage. Besides, old Bob's bellow was really starting to grate and despite all Dave's pleading the man refused to pipe down. Once the old bellower started regaling the bar with the story of 'the strange death of the vicar' in the Fifties Harry knew it was time to take his leave.

He'd been hearing the tale all his life, of Edward, the old vicar, and the thing that came for him on a stormy night. As a lad he and his pals had spent many hours, in the rain, in the graveyard, looking for said dog, but all they'd got was wet and cold, and

Harry had long since dismissed the tale as just another in a long line of local stories put forward by the church to keep the peasants under control. Harry had never been one for 'churching', despite being dragged to Sunday School, then Sunday Services every weekend, and having to suffer through R.E. classes at school... all that, a grandmother who read nothing but the bible and never spared the rod... and none of it took. While the rest of the village life revolved round the doings at the church and vicarage, Harry's was a firm circle between the pub and the sheep. He knew which one he'd always preferred, and never regretted a day of it.

Besides, he had more than enough to be worrying about in the real world today. If there was a big fairy in the sky directing the traffic, it was doing a piss-poor job of it today. The rain was getting worse if anything, being driven by a strengthening north wind he had to lean against to make headway, and the river was up at least another foot. It had burst its banks in a long swathe across his lower field, submerging an area the size of a football pitch in dank, muddy swirls. Despite the inclement weather there was something mesmerizing about the ebb and flow of the water, and he dallied for several minutes watching it, realising as he did so that the rise in water level was noticeable, even minute to minute. Maybe that blowhard Bob was finally onto something after all.

If this keeps up we're going to be in big trouble.

It was trouble due to flooding that was big in his mind; he hadn't been thinking about much else as he pushed back through the wind to the farm. It was only as he got close to the big barn that he realized there were other kinds of trouble he should be worried about.

He was in the lee of the building, finally getting some protection from the wind, when he heard it; squeals which told him straight away that his flock were in trouble. It was far more than a concerned bleating, these were high, animal screams, sounds he never knew sheep were capable of making. Something thudded, hard, against the corrugated metal sheeting to his left, shaking the whole wall. The screaming went up a notch, matching the wail of the wind and he heard frantic scurrying from inside. There was another squealing scream, one that was cut off as quickly as if a needle had been raised from a vinyl record.

Something's in there with them.

He ran for the barn door, but just as he reached it the quality of the sound changed again, from wild screaming to piteous bleating, then, more ominously, all noise from inside fell quiet, leaving the wind to scream alone. He smelled something rank, wet hair, bad meat, nothing that smelled like sheep.

He opened the door and stepped inside, not into a barn, but to a slaughterhouse.

- DUFFIELD -

Wiggo was far from happy when shown the letter. They had deplaned and piled into a 4x4, hurrying to stow their gear against the rain that was lashing hard from the north. Now they were all safely inside and shut off from the weather. Duffield had passed the note back to the sergeant.

"George? The auld fella fae yon London job with The Blob? The man wi' the beer and the hollow legs? That's who's got us playing in this pish? That George?"

"Aye, that George," Duffield said. "I thought he was a nice old duffer."

"The job was done by the time you got involved though. He was a good man for the ale, I'll give you that," Wiggo replied, waving the letter. "But this is more of that kind of shite auld Seton liked to get us involved in... fucking black magic, auld wive's tales, spooks and bogles and nowt you can get to fuck off with a bullet and harsh language. Mark my words, this is going to be a right load of old bollocks, right from the start."

"I do like a positive minded sergeant," Duffield said, and laughed but didn't get one in reply from Wiggo, who was still complaining as the 4x4 drove off into the rain.

"Fuckin' big black ghostly dugs. That's all we fucking need."

At least Wiggo was in the back with Mac so out of direct earshot. Wilkins was up front in the passenger seat, acting as Duffield's navigator. They'd landed at a small civilian airfield about thirty miles from their destination, loaded their gear in the ample room in the back end, and now were wending their way through an ever narrowing series of country roads, edging closer to Titmarsh even as the rain washed in waves over them. It turned the roads into shallow streams and threatened to overwhelm the wipers, which, even on full, were having trouble maintaining a clear field of view. Duffield felt a headache coming on.

"If I was a big black dug I wouldn't be out in shite like this," Wiggo said from the back.

"If you were a big black dug you'd be lying in front of a fire licking your balls and eating biscuits, Sarge," Wilkins replied.

"Don't mock it until you've tried it, lad," Wiggo said and the resultant laughter kept the weather at bay for at least a minute until a gust of wind rocked the vehicle from side to side and the back end slid away for a worrying couple of seconds before Duffield got it going in a straight line.

"How much farther did you say?" he asked. "I'm only asking because this is getting oan ma tits."

"Should be a bridge coming up any time now, boss," Wilkins replied, holding the map close to his face and peering at it. "The village is on the far side of that."

The bridge came into view seconds later, but there was a yellow and red double barrier across it, reflective red lights

25

showing brilliant back at them in their headlights. Duffield slowed cautiously, aware of the danger of hydroplaning in the surface water that covered the roadway. A very wet-looking, very young, police constable flagged them down to the side of the road.

Duffield wound down his window enough to talk, getting a wash of rain in his face in the process.

"Can't let you through here I'm afraid, sir. It's not safe," the constable said. "The river's in spate and the bridge could go at any time."

"Any way we can go round?"

"If you're not heading for Titmarsh itself, yes. Back up two miles, take the first on the left and it'll get you back on the main road."

"No can do. We need to get to the village," Duffield said. "Official business."

The constable looked at them and their vehicle as if really seeing them for the first time and pulled the barrier aside before waving them through. The SUV sloshed through ankle-deep water across to the other side where another cop, a woman this time, was waiting. She didn't look any less wet.

Duffield wound down the window again as she approached.

"You were quick," she said. "We only phoned half an hour ago."

Duffield got out of the car to talk to her; it didn't seem fair to let her get soaked all alone.

26

"I think we're at cross purposes here. Whoever you're expecting, we're not it. We're here on M.O.D. business, to talk to the old lady at the vicarage."

"M.O.D. is it? Talk is it?" she said, looking Duffield up and down. "You don't look like a man who's much for talking. So you're not here about Harry's sheep?"

"Not unless they're in the vicarage," Duffield replied, and at least got a thin smile in reply.

"I'm sure you know what you're doing, but Eleanor is half-senile and what the M.O.D. might want with her is something I don't have time to be thinking about right now. You won't get much sense from her in any case. But I'm Jenny," she said, putting out a hand. "I'm what passes for the law in the village. If you and your team plan on doing anything daft around here, I'd appreciate a heads-up first. You'll find the vicarage at the highest point in town; probably the best place to be for the next few hours."

Duffield had a look behind him. The river under the bridge ran in full spate, only inches below the top of the old stone archway of the main span. Muddy water leaked around the edge on top where the bank was nearest the roadway.

"Will it hold?"

She shook her head.

"Not unless the rain stops right now. Even then we're still a couple of hours from high tide and when this lot backs up it's not just the bridge we'll have to worry about. It might be good news you're here; if evacuation is needed I'll be looking for all the help I can get. Don't go far," she said, and laughed. "In joke, I'm afraid. There's not any far to go to around here when it gets like this. If you need lodgings, head for the pub, and tell Dave I sent you."

"And if you need us, that's probably where we'll be," Duffield replied. "But I hope to be in and out of here quickly."

"Trust me," she said, "The only thing that's going to happen quickly around here is this river rising. So if you've got business, best get to it."

Duffield got back in the car and left her standing in the rain. He wondered who else she was expecting, and what sheep might have to do with it, but put that to the back of his mind. He had enough to think about just trying to keep on the road which was now more of a fast-running stream.

The rain continued to lash down. When they reached the small, neat, central square of the village the only thing he could see were the lights and signage of the pub.

"So what's it to be, lads," he said, "vicarage or bar first?"

It wasn't a tough decision to make given the weather which appeared to ramp up even more as they parked in front of the old inn. They left all their gear in the back for now, Duffield ensuring the vehicle was secure before following the others inside.

The bar felt warm, cosy and welcoming as soon as he got through the door, which was more than could be said for the cold stares they were getting from some of the patrons.

"Look, lads," Wiggo said loudly and disdainfully. "It's wan o' them local bars for local people. Whose sheep do I have to shag to get a drink around here?"

At least the barman laughed at that, but an old chap at the far end of the bar looked about to take umbrage, so Duffield stepped up quickly to talk to the barman.

"The police officer at the bridge said you have rooms?"

"That was no officer, that was my wife," the man replied with a laugh. "But she was right. Four is it? Or two doubles?"

"We'll take four," Wiggo replied. "The M.O.D. can afford it."

The old chap at the end of the bar's ears pricked up at that.

"M.O.D. is it? What in blazes are you doing here in a storm? Some kind of black ops shit I expect? Or is this something to do with Harry's sheep?"

"What is it with you people and sheep?" Wiggo said, and might have continued if Duffield hadn't stopped him with a glare.

Duffield addressed the barman.

"We're here at the request of an interested party to speak to the old lady at the vicarage," he said. The barman nodded, as if it was an everyday occurrence to have the military turn up in his bar looking to speak to a ninety year old woman. The old chap wasn't so sanguine.

"Eleanor? She's addled, just like everybody else around here," he cackled. "Ye'll get no sense from her, mark my words."

The barman replied wearily.

"Bob, you've been warned. If you chase off any more of my custom, I'm putting you out in the rain."

The older man grinned, but at least went quiet and went back to sipping at a pint.

Duffield came to a decision. He tossed the SUV keys to Wiggo.

"Get yourself and the lads settled in and get the kit out of the car. Then you can have a pint."

"What about you, boss?"

"I'm off to see a woman about a dug."

- HARRY -

Harry Greenfield sat at his kitchen table, a glass of whisky in his left hand, his right holding the stock of his twelve-bore which lay stretched across the table in front of him. His hands had stopped shaking now that the shock had abated, but he knew the sight that had awaited him in the barn would always be there hereafter in the back of his mind; it wasn't something anyone could forget in a hurry, no matter how much he tried to get whisky to wash it away.

Slaughterhouse wasn't a big enough word to describe it. Harry had never been a sentimentalist about his flock; it had always been his belief that a good farmer couldn't afford to be. But seeing them torn and bloody and strewn to the four corners of the barn like so many discarded scraps of meat had brought him literally to his knees in tears. He knelt there, trousers soaking up blood to mix with the rain, his gaze falling on details he knew were engraving themselves into his skull; a wet rib cage here, a back leg that had been torn from a body there, bloody threads of muscle and fat gleaming, and there, a pile of torsos and bones, as if left as a totem, his old ram's head, horns raised above a skinned skull from which the eyes had been forcibly torn, leaving just two bloody, black holes dripping gore to stare into Harry's soul.

He'd only staggered away when the stench assaulted his breathing passages and brought on a gag reflex that forced him to stand, stagger outside, and throw up his bar lunch by the side of the door.

He barely remembered making an incoherent call to the police. Jenny had come out herself, taken one look at the carnage, and almost thrown up atop the mess he'd left. She was made of strong stuff though, and she'd actually gone inside the barn for a close look at the nature of the damage done, a thing that Harry couldn't manage to face.

"Who the fuck would do a thing like this?" she said when she came out, but Harry had no answer for her; he had no words left in him, only pain.

She'd led him gently back to the farmhouse, and they'd both had a quick stiffener from his whisky bottle before she spent ten minutes just sitting with him, more to ensure he was okay than in any realistic attempt to do something about the dead beasts. She put a cold hand over his, as if petting an old dog.

"We'll get them, Harry. We'll get the bastards who did this."

Harry heard her, but the words were meaningless, not registering in a mind that was too full of an image of a peeled ram's skull, dead eyes staring.

Finally she'd stood and left him alone with his grief. He'd sat at the kitchen table with another large whisky while she called up the local council, then the Ministry of Agriculture. Harry heard her speaking but took none of it in; his head was full of nothing but a roaring wail of terror that echoed in all his empty places and the vision of the staring skull.

Once she was done on the phone Jenny took his face in her hands and softly told him somebody was going to be sent to investigate, and that he shouldn't do anything daft in the meantime. Then she'd left, although he scarcely noticed her absence.

So here he was, doing nothing daft, waiting for someone to come and explain things to him in a way he might be able to understand. And if whoever, or whatever, turned up wasn't who he was expecting? Well, that's what the 12-bore was for.

Payment for the sheep was required.

And somebody would be paying in full.

He was vaguely aware that some time had passed; the level of whisky in the bottle had dropped for one thing. The howl of wind outside had intensified, the rain hitting the old kitchen window like a manic drummer obsessed with the snare drum and the old oak door rattling in its frame on the backbeat. But something else had brought him up from wherever he'd been wool-gathering, something out of place in the memory-managed internal model he held of the farm he'd lived in all his life.

There it was again, a scratching, as of nails against stone, coming from outside the window, loud even above the wind and rain. It wasn't mice, nor even rats; he knew their small sounds only too well from long experience. No, this was something different, a stranger to the house.

I hear you, you bastard. You don't sound like you're the man from the Ministry.

He reached for the shotgun. The scratching stopped as his finger curled around the trigger. There was only the sonic blast of the storm as he headed for the kitchen door, but he closed up the shotgun, locked and both barrels loaded, and kept it raised as he bent forward and turned the handle. He'd seen the damage wrought on his animals. If that could be done to the old ram, it could just as quickly be done to a man. He wasn't about to let anybody try.

As soon as the lock cleared the latch the door blew open with a crash that rattled all the dishes in the dresser on the opposite wall, the force of it almost throwing him off balance. He raised the shotgun, expecting an attack, but got only rain in his face for his sins as the wind howled around him. He stood in the doorway, defying the elements, screaming out into the storm.

"Come on then. What the fuck are you waiting for? Christmas?"

He got no answer, just more rain, more wind… more misery.

It was impossible to see more than ten yards in the lashing rain and the wind threatened to knock him off his feet with every gust. He was soaked through again, as if he'd been wading deep in a pool of water, and the rain felt like hail against his cheeks. But in the end it was the call of the bottle that got him moving. He turned back, had to fight with the door to get it closed against a wind insistent on keeping it open, and returned to his chair, and to the whisky.

He'd only been sitting down for a minute when the scratching started   again.

- DUFFIELD -

Duffield was starting to think that Wiggo might have been right about the merits of this job after all.

After a short but very wet walk up from the pub, where his waterproofs mainly kept the water on the outside where it should be, the vicarage itself was cosy enough, if a little too on the nose as an old-lady-in-an-English-village stereotype. The fittings were well-polished brass and old wood, tables and chairbacks were draped in intricate lace doilies and shawls, and faded portraits of long passed family shared wall space with rural and pastoral scenes in dark, earthy oils. Everything smelled of lavender and polish, and even a lone cobweb up in the corner of the old beam rafters looked neat and tidy.

The elderly housekeeper who introduced him to Eleanor was all politeness and efficiency and had already retreated to the back of the cottage somewhere to give him privacy in his chat with the lady of the house in a parlour that looked like it hadn't changed much in fifty years or more.

But Eleanor herself was proving to be hard work. It wasn't that she was 'addled', as the old boy in the bar had inferred, it was just that she had a magpie mind, always distracted by the next bit of shiny, and getting information out of her was like drawing blood from a stone. He'd already learned more than he would ever need about the Titmarsh Ladies Sewing Circle, the infamous history of Bob, the auld lad from the bar, and the terrible state of the country compared to 'the Good Old Days'. He was still no nearer any details of the reason why he had come. He only started to get somewhere when he mentioned George.

"Ah, George," she said, and suddenly Duffield caught a glimpse of the girl she must have been. "I thought he was the one... weddings and babies and little Georges and Eleanors running around the vicarage. That would have been fun. But it wasn't to be. Father's death put an end to all of that. How do you know George? He's my age."

Duffield approached the subject slowly.

"I met him in London a few years back, and he's asked me to speak to you as a favor to him."

"You've talked to him? I thought he must have passed years ago."

"Last time we spoke he was hale and hearty. He's worried about you though, and sent me a letter asking me to look you up, and for you to tell me the story of the black dog."

He handed her the letter. Tears ran down her cheeks as she read it, and her eyes were watery pools when she handed the pages back to him.

"Yes. That's how it was. That's exactly how it was. Old George," she said absently. "He was a card and a half. He saw it too, you know? It's not all just in my head."

Duffield nodded, but didn't speak; she had that look in her eye, the one that told him a tale was coming, and he knew from youthful experience with two voluble Great Aunts that old ladies, when they got to the right point, should just be allowed to tell their own stories in their own time. One wrong word now and all he'd get was more tales of the Sewing Circle. He sipped at a cup of too-sweet tea and waited.

As expected, she began by taking the long way round.

"I should have married George," she said. "It wasn't as if he didn't ask me, several times. But Father's death had stricken me so sore I couldn't think of anything else, and by the time I noticed George wasn't there, he really wasn't there, off and away and doing his science things with his science friends and with me left to look after the vicarage."

She sighed and patted away a tear.

"And it's all that bloody dog's fault."

Even the mild swear word sounded somewhat shocking coming from her, but she was getting into it now, and Duffield was trying not to catch her eye lest he distract her.

"It all came to a head three weeks after George's visit, after the things he described in that letter. He'd told me about seeing the dog on the edge of the field... back then he told me everything, but duty had called and he'd had to go to London. Meanwhile Father was getting ever more distraught, convinced his end was nigh, and had taken to spending most of his spare time on his knees in the chapel, praying. That's where I found him, one night when I took him a spot of supper.

"I was about to ask after his well-being when I saw in his eyes that he was scared... no, worse than that, he was terrified.

"'It will be tonight, my dear,' he said. 'Can't you hear it?'

"All I could hear was the howl of the wind and the sound of rain on the windows, for it was a filthy night, much like tonight. I told him as much, but he was having none of it.

"I was about to exhort him to return with me to the house when the door of the chapel banged, hard, in its frame, rattling the hinges, and a howl filled the air. It was most definitely not the wind."

She stopped speaking, and looked Duffield directly in the eye.

"You're a practical lad, I can see that, no nonsense for you. So you probably won't believe this next bit, but I'll swear on any number of bibles you want that it's true, and I'm a vicar's daughter, so you know what that means to me."

"I might be up for more nonsense than you know," Duffield said and smiled, but didn't get one in reply, for she was immediately back to the story.

"The chapel went cold, as if a sudden frost had fallen over it.

"'It's here,' Father whispered, and pointed.

"A grey mist rose near the altar and started to form and blacken. Twin red coals glowed at head height and... I don't know how to say this without you thinking me daft, so I'll just say it... the figure of the great hound coalesced and thickened in front of us. The candles on the altar flickered wildly, threatening to puff out completely.

"The black dog prowled around the altar and font, watching us, as if trying to gauge our intent. I can tell you, my only thought was a fear that gripped at my heart, threatening to stop it completely.

"The beast now seemed totally physical and present in the chapel. Its chest moved as it panted, and I smelled the wet, animalistic odor of it, heard its feet pad softly on the flagstones; there was no doubt it was there, and yet there was also something of the ethereal about it, something definitely not of this world.

"'Repeat after me,' Father said. 'You'll know the words.'

"He launched into Latin.

"'*Dómine, exáudi oratiónem méam. Et clámor meus ad te véniatn nomini et virtute. Domini nostri Jesu Christi, eradicare et effugare a Dei Ecclesia, ab animabus ad imaginem Dei conditis ac pretioso divini Agni sanguini redemptis.*'

"The dog raised its snout and howled. The rafters of the old chapel shivered and the candles flickered wildly once more, casting dancing shadows around the room. Beside me Father frantically muttered in Latin, all the while staring at the floor and making the sign of the cross at his chest. I raised my voice again to join him as he lifted his head and declaimed loudly.

"'*In nomini et virtute Domini nostri Jesu Christi.*'

"The dog began to lose cohesion, its hind quarters fading and wraith-like. The power of our Lord was working against it... or so I hoped.

"*'Váde sátana, invéntor et magíster ómnis falláciae, hóstis humánae salútis. Da lócum Christo, in quo níhil invenísti de opéribus tuis; da lócum Ecclésia Uni, Sanctae, Cathólicae, et Apostólicae, quam Christus ípse acquisívit sánguine suo.'*

"The dog became even more transparent; I could see the wall of the chapel through it. But I was to be given no cause for celebration, for at that very moment the chapel door was thrown open. Mother strode in, took one look at the now spectral black dog, and began to scream the place down. There wasn't much left of Shuck but a head and the two red coals of its eyes by this point.

"But it was enough.

"Father shouted out, *'adjurámus te per Déum vívum, per Déum vérum, per Déum sánctum'* but his last word was cut off as if all breath had been taken from him.

"I felt it pass me like a stiff, cold breeze smelling of wet hair and old meat. It latched every bit of what remained of itself full onto Father's face.

"Father took one, last, deep breath, clutched at his chest, and fell at my feet, dead eyes staring up at me.

"There was nothing remaining of Black Shuck but a smoke-like wisp of grey in the air that dissipated as Mother ran forward, still screaming.

"She was answered by one, single, mournful howl, fading fast, as Shuck left the chapel, its dark work done."

It had all come out of her in a rush at the end, as if she'd been saving it up to tell somebody, and now it was done the tears came, running unnoticed down both her cheeks, her eyes still looking at something elsewhere, elsewhen. Duffield refrained from commenting for a long minute, during which time the old lady made an obvious effort and pulled herself together. She took a silk handkerchief trimmed with fine lace from her sleeve and dabbed daintily at her eyes, as if afraid they might break if touched too roughly. She made the handkerchief vanish again before continuing.

"For the long count of years since then I thought that was the end of it. A new vicar came in but he liked to live over in Norwich and didn't stay in the village. It's his son that's here now, but he too is mostly an out-of-towner, which is probably for the best on a night like this. The people of the village were good enough to let first mother and me, and then, after she passed, me on my own stay on in the vicarage rather than having it sitting empty. Here I have been this long count of years, like an old Hobbit in her hole. It's not been a great life, but it has been a quiet one. Mostly. Until last month. That's when I started hearing it."

"Shuck?"

There were more tears in her eyes when she looked up at Duffield again and nodded.

"It's back. Every day it creeps closer.

"And this time it has come for me."

- WIGGO -

Wiggo had begun to enjoy himself.

He still wasn't quite convinced about the new lieutenant. The lad had come good in a tight spot on that job down the big cave... saved the captain's life more than once when Banks' gammy leg betrayed him. But he was young, and had a bit of cockiness to him that reminded Wiggo too much of his younger self. Plus he had big boots to fill, and in Wiggo's view was never going to be able to pull off the casual aura of confidence and efficiency that the captain had always carried around with him like a favourite shirt.

On the other hand, any boss who let his team loose in a pub and buggered off to leave them to it couldn't be all bad. Now Wiggo was on his second pint, as were Wilkins and Mac, and Wiggo was just about ready for some serious piss-taking.

He'd even picked out his target as the miserable auld git at the far end of the bar who'd made the black ops' crack when they arrived. Wiggo was just about to start working on him when the police officer the lieutenant had talked to on the bridge came in. She was a soaking wet mess, but her tone was firm as she shouted across the bar.

"I need some muscle and I need it fast."

"Now there's an offer I can't refuse," Wiggo replied loudly, then remembered, too late, that the cop was also the barman's wife. "Sorry, man," he said sheepishly. "I've got a mouth that runs faster than my brain."

The barman laughed.

"There's a lot of that about. Must be something in the beer."

"Did you not hear me?" the policewoman said, louder. "I need help, right fucking now. The bridge is out, we're cut off from everybody else, and the river is still rising. Stop pissing about and come with me, or you'll not have a bar left to be a wanker in."

She gave Wiggo and the others just enough time to retrieve their waterproofs from their rooms then, with her husband in tow, led them out into the storm.

Wiggo started to head for the SUV but she pulled him by the arm.

"We won't be needing that. It'd be no use to you anyway, where we're going."

Lieutenant Duffield arrived just as they were heading downwards into what was more of a river than a street.

"What's going on?" the officer asked.

"I've press-ganged your lads," Jenny shouted. "We need all hands on deck, and we need them now."

Wiggo had to give the new boss credit for not pulling rank, or wasting time with questions. Instead Duffield just nodded.

"Just tell us what's needed," he shouted back. "We'll do what we can."

She nodded her thanks then turned away, setting a fast pace. They followed her down the road. The inn and small village square sat at almost the highest point of the village, only the vicarage, church hall and chapel occupying slightly higher ground. Elsewhere all the ground sloped away. In the direction they were headed it led them past cottages on either side then to a flat area set up for both football and rugby, although there wasn't going to be much of either played there for a while. The whole playing surface was already awash with water. Just beyond the rugby goal posts Wiggo saw a line of men frantically piling up sandbags along the rim of what was obviously the riverbank. It looked like they were already fighting a losing battle.

It was pretty obvious what was required. The sandbags were being ferried in on tractors and trailers, and there was frantic work to be done, unloading and piling bags in the face of a still rapidly rising river.

Wiggo and the others joined the line. He was nearest to the growing wall, the last of the squad to get a bag. He swung it from his left side to his right, passing it on at waist height to a burly farmhand who looked as strong as an ox but also as tired as any man Wiggo had ever seen. He had a four foot high wall of sandbags in front of him, and hauled each new bag up on top of that, grunting with effort each time. The river lapped at the top and spilled over in several places not ten yards to the right of them, hungry for its freedom. If the bags didn't hold, the men working on the wall were liable to be swept away with any breach that occurred.

Rain and wind lashed hard in their faces, the bags seemed as heavy as if they were packed with cement rather than sand, and still the river rose implacably just past their makeshift wall. Wiggo had been made to work hard on training exercises over the years but this had all of them beat for sheer effort and strength of will required not to buckle. It was obvious to Wiggo they were working in a lost cause, but the lad at the wall was fighting to protect his home, it was the least Wiggo could do to stand by him.

It seemed to go on forever. He got into the routine easily enough, fetching and swinging each bag as smoothly as he could manage, but the rain and wind was relentless, and his shoulders soon ached with dull pain that he knew would be with him for many hours, if not days ahead. The big man to his left was noticeably flagging now; the wall was five feet high and each bag had to be lifted higher than the previous. He wasn't going to be able to get much higher. The river lapped over the bags just to the north of them in an ever growing stream.

And still they piled them on. And still the rain beat relentlessly down on them. The river kept rising.

Something had to give, and finally, inevitably, it did.

"It's going to go," somebody shouted. "Everybody back."

Even then the big farmer wouldn't shift. He tugged the last bag off Wiggo and threw it double-handed on top of the rest.

"Another. Right fucking now," he shouted in Wiggo's face, but Wiggo had nothing to give him; the line had disbanded and everyone else was already heading at speed for higher ground.

"Come on, big man, time to go," Wiggo said, then saw with dismay it was too late. The wall behind the farmer buckled beneath the pressure and a wall of water burst through it.

The big man just stood and looked at it, as if amazed that all his efforts had come so quickly to naught. Wiggo grabbed him by the arm and, not daring to look back, turned and ran. Within seconds water sloshed around his ankles, his knees, his thighs, and they would have been swept off their feet if it hadn't been for the big man's brute strength. Even then they had to give way to the flow of water somewhat just to make some headway against it, and were being pushed south, away from where the others had already reached the higher ground. The flow threatened to drag them back towards the river, and Wiggo knew there would be no coming back from that. He kept his gaze on a tangled copse of straggly birch trees ahead of them, and dragged the farmer with him towards what he hoped would be safety.

"One big push, big man. If we get to the trees we're nearly home and dry. I might even buy you a pint."

"Make it two and you're on," the lad shouted, and put on a surprising burst of speed, dragging Wiggo along with him even though the water by now was almost up to their waists. Despite his efforts at the wall building, the lad still appeared as strong as ox, as if the thought of beer had spurred him into a burst of energy. Wiggo wasn't about to argue and, holding tight to the back of the big farmer's jacket, did what he could to help them along, although it was obvious they were fighting a losing cause; the strength of the flow against them was too great to be resisted for much longer. Wiggo had visions of him thinking more of bear than dog. The weight of it threw Wiggo aside, only his grip on the tree preventing him from being tumbled headlong into the torrent. A fresh wash of water threatened to wash him away completely, his shoulder muscles squealing in pain as he fought against the pull.them being swept away and off to a watery grave, but the big man had other ideas.

"Fuck this shit," he bellowed, and with one swift movement turned, lifted Wiggo bodily as if he was no more than one of the sandbags, and threw him towards the trees. Wiggo hardly had time to process what happened. One second he'd been treading water, the next he was flying through the air. He landed, hard, back against a sapling, feeling wood break under his weight even as water rushed around his legs. He turned, grabbed a tree trunk and locked his hands around it, hanging on for grim death.

"Get over here, lad," he shouted over his shoulder. "It's our only hope."

When he turned his head he saw that the farmer was almost ashore, arm stretched out looking for help. Wiggo let go of the tree with one hand and reached for him.

Their fingertips brushed against each other.

"Got you," Wiggo said.

He smelled the thing that came out of the copse from behind him before he saw it; wet hair and old meat. Heat radiated off it as itf barreled past him, something big that had

Behind him something growled, someone screamed and there was a crunching sound the likes of which Wiggo hoped never to have to hear again. When he turned back to look at the flowing water there was only the flood. The big man, and whatever the fuck that thing was that had come out of the copse, were nowhere to be seen.

The water kept rising.

- HARRY -

Harry only realised how much trouble he was in when he saw dirty water come in an inch-high wave under the farmhouse door. He never thought that the farm itself might be in danger of flooding; it sat a good ten feet above any previous high water mark. Indeed, it had been built in its place by Harry's grandfather for the express purpose of keeping it safe from any rise in the river.

"Keep your feet dry and your throat wet and you'll have a happy life," he remembered the old man saying. Harry couldn't have been more than six at the time, but it had been in this same room, at this same table. Harry had been managing the wet throat part just fine on his own for years now, but he was failing the dry feet part badly; dirty water was sloshing around the toes of his boots.

He'd been dozing, lost in a whisky-induced haze, and more than a third of the kitchen had water flowing over the stone floor before he even noticed. By the time he stood, unsteady at first before adrenalin cleared his head, half the floor was awash.

Even slightly addled with booze as he was, he wasn't stupid enough to open the door; a sudden wall of water wasn't what he needed right now. He hefted the shotgun, not ready to abandon it, and made for the back door, even as the front door squealed and creaked, rebelling against the weight of water that must be pushing against it from outside.

If it goes before I get out of here, I've had it.

He sloshed through the hallway and the main living area, feet splashing on sodden carpet. The exposed timbers in the ceiling overhead creaked and groaned as if fit to split and the floor shifted, like a boat rocking in a storm. Harry put on a burst of speed, raising splashes around his ankles up to his knees.

His opening of the back door coincided with the front door giving way. Harry went outside into the full face of the storm with a wave of water coursing through the farmhouse at his back.

The backyard of the farm was on a slight upward slope, and that was the only thing that saved him as he ran up it, gasping for air as the rain tried to fill his mouth and nostrils, the water tapping at his heels as he reached the high point of the top field above the farmhouse.

Where the footpath leading to town had been was now the banks of a fast flowing spate, the river, more than ten feet higher than it had been just hours earlier, was a mucky brown, foaming force of chaos, and when Harry turned back to look at the farmhouse he was just in time to see first the front wall collapse, then the whole structure, house, barn and outbuildings, all crumple together as if squeezed in a giant fist before being swept down to join the other debris being carried along by the flood. Within seconds nothing remained to show that the farm had ever existed.

Rain and wind blew in his face, soaking him through his jumper and trousers in seconds, the chill already reaching for his bones.

Got to get somewhere dry and warm, out of this shite. And quickly.

But with the footpath out of commission, the only way was to try to make a path through the fields alongside, and they were even more sodden than Harry himself. His feet sucked in mud, his shoes feeling as if they'd taken on a load of cement, and every step was a trudge that drained strength out of him.

He had his wallet in his back pocket, the scant few clothes he was wearing, and the shotgun, both barrels loaded. Everything else he had ever been, everything his family had ever been, was now somewhere else, lost to the flood, and he was a keeper without a flock.

What am I going to do with myself now?

He answered himself quickly.

You'll be doing fuck all if you don't get out of this weather sharpish.

He had no other options open. He put his head down, and put one foot after the other, heading, he hoped, towards the village.

He was aware of nothing but wind and rain and ever thickening mud underfoot. He had kept the still-rising river on his right hand side so far, but had to come to a halt as he approached what had been the sports-field. The level ground was now a new lake, one that was getting bigger by the second.

He hadn't been thinking big enough and now he saw it in his mind's eye; if the water kept rising the way it was going, the village wasn't going to be a place of safety, it was going to be an island amid a flood, and one that was going to be getting ever smaller. But he had no other options open; with the water this high the bridge to the south out of town would be out already. The only other egress was two miles back the way he'd just come, and he already knew that too was flooded.

It's the village or nothing.

He turned to his left, hoping there was going to be enough time to skirt the new lake before his path to the village was completely cut off in front of him.

The water kept rising.

- DUFFIELD -

Duffield found Wiggo more by luck than judgement.

They'd seen the two stragglers struggling in the torrent. The remaining members of the squad, with the policewoman and her husband with them, had tried to head in that direction but were cut off from following by sheer volume of water. They'd been forced to skirt around the back of a copse of straggly birch trees, and when they finally managed to circumnavigate the trees they arrived at a flooded roadway that was now another part of the rising spate. There was nothing to see but foaming brown water, and no sign of either man. The new branch of the river that had overwhelmed the playing fields was still rising steadily.

The policewoman tugged at Duffield's arm.

"We've lost them. There's others that still need our help."

Duffield wasn't ready to bail on a squad member.

I hope I'm never ready.

"They've gone, man," the barman said, shouting above the wind. "And so will we be if we stay here much longer."

Duffield refused to give up. He pushed his way through the copse of saplings, wet leaves and branches lashing against his cheeks and slapping on his waterproofs. There was still no sign of the missing men. He'd almost reached the water's edge, and was finally about to turn back when he caught a glimpse of something paler ahead, almost white against the muddy water beyond.

He stepped over, and looked down to see Wiggo, only his head and arms above water, the flow already tugging urgently at his body below his chest. The man looked exhausted, his face drawn and haggard, his knuckles bone-white where his hands gripped the thin trunk of a sapling that was miraculously holding firm against the flood.

"Need some help here," he shouted, but didn't wait to see if there was any reply.

He had to force his way through more birch branches, and then stand in the raging water up to his thighs, before he could find a place where he could try to lift Wiggo out of where he was lodged. Wilko and Mac arrived at his back, but there was no room for all three of them to get close to where Wiggo lay.

He bent and grabbed Wiggo under the shoulders. The sergeant's eyes fluttered and he groaned, but didn't rise out of unconsciousness, even when tugged bodily out of the tangle of trees and branches. Duffield took the weight, then needed Wilkins and Mac to form a chain to avoid both of them getting washed away, his every muscle straining to hold firm against the current. He had a couple of bad moments where he thought he was gone, feet momentarily lifted off the bottom by the flood, but then Mac grabbed him by the waist, Wilkins grabbed Mac and with Wiggo in tow all four of them fell forward, out of the edge of the copse and onto sodden ground at the feet of Jenny and Dave.

"Big John? Any sign of Big John?" Jenny said, and Duffield guessed that must be the farmer, but he could only shake his head, still trying to catch his breath after the effort.

The policewoman bent and shouted in Wiggo's face.

"Where the fuck is he? Where's the big man?"

Wiggo's eyes fluttered again and his fingers twitched but that was the extent of his answer. Duffield gently moved the policewoman aside.

"I'll get this one back to someplace warm," he said, still gasping for breath. "Wilkins and Mac here will go with you to look for your man." He turned to Wilkins. "If he's anywhere, he's going to be downstream. Help her look... but don't be doing anything stupid. We've got one man down already and we only just got here."

He bent to Wiggo and, after two attempts, got him up in a fireman's lift.

Dave the barman offered to help but Duffield brushed him off.

"No. You're needed to look for your man. Is the bar locked up?"

Dave nodded, but handed Duffield the keys.

"Just don't drink it dry before I get back. But the whisky is on me, and there's plenty of it."

Duffield left the others heading south along the still rising river and set his sights on the lights of the village up the slope. Wiggo felt like a dead weight over his shoulder. Duffield muttered under his breath.

"Don't you fucking dare die on me, Wiggo. Don't you fucking dare."

He'd trained carrying heavy backpacks up steep hills, but somehow the rain and wind made Wiggo feel twice as heavy again, and he felt every step of the way in the muscles of his legs and back. By the time he reached the village square he was sweating heavily inside his clothes and his breath came in heaving gulps. Negotiating the door handle proved tricky and he nearly dropped Wiggo but saved the fall by ramming them both tight into one corner while reaching out and pulling the handle down. The door swung inward and he staggered inside, almost knocking over a tall coat stand in the process and had to take a second to steady himself. It was relatively plain sailing after that.

He managed to fumble his way into the main part of the empty bar without dropping Wiggo on the floor, but couldn't find a light switch. It felt warm and cozy inside though, so Duffield settled for dumping the sergeant in a corner seat, and making sure he wasn't going to fall over before leaving to go in search of the promised whisky in the gloom of the bar area.

By the time he got back Wiggo's eyes were partially open, and the sergeant was trying to speak. Duffield shushed him by the simple expedient of putting an opened bottle of Scotch in his hand, which Wiggo took to with gusto before sputtering a mouthful of it out over the table in front of him and breaking into a hacking cough.

"Fuck, I need a fag," the sergeant muttered.

"Now I know you're going to be okay," Duffield replied with a laugh as Wiggo looked around him, confused. Duffield took the whisky bottle and knocked back a swig, giving it back to Wiggo before he was tempted to take more.

"How the fuck did I get here?" Wiggo said.

"Over my shoulder," Duffield replied. "The others are still down by the river, searching for the big man. Did you see what happened to him?"

Wiggo's brows furrowed and his eyes darkened.

"Smelled it, heard it, saw it," he said, "That auld bastard George might have been onto something after all, boss."

"It was a dog?"

"If it was a dog it was the biggest fucker you've ever seen. Might even be a bear for all I ken. Something big, hairy and pissed off in any case. And it smells like warm shite."

"And the big lad?"

Wiggo shook his head and was about to say more when the bell above the door jingled and the others all arrived in a bunch. The barman turned on the lights as they entered. Duffield could tell by their faces that their search had not gone well.

The policewoman headed immediately for Wiggo.

"You're going to tell me what happened, and you're going to tell me right fucking now."

"The big man saved my life," Wiggo said quietly. "Picked me up and threw me out of the water and into the trees like I weighed no more than a babbie."

"Then what?" the policewoman said. Duffield could see that she was furious, ready to hit something and not very particular about what. "You just fucking left him to drown?"

Wiggo looked at Duffield, who gave a nod.

"Tell her the truth, Wiggo. She deserves to know."

"You're fucking right I deserve to know. And I want to know right fucking now."

Wiggo took a deep slug from the whisky bottle before answering.

"I tried to reach him. Nearly got him too, and would have done but the big dug got him," he said baldly. "Came out of the trees like a fucking grizzly bear and before I could even move it had him, off and away and into the water. Did you find him?"

The policewoman looked grim, but the anger was already washing away as quickly as it had come as Wiggo's words sunk in and a memory came for her.

"We found what's left of him. He looked like he'd been put through a combine harvester. One of his legs was torn off completely, and the rest of him was stuffed up tight under the stanchions of an electricity pylon, as if he'd been shoved in there to be kept for later. First Harry's sheep, now this? What the fuck is going on here?"

She turned to Duffield.

"And what the fuck do you know you're not telling me?"

Duffield took the whisky bottle from Wiggo and took another slug for himself before replying.

"The simplest thing is to show you what brought us here," he said, and took old George's letter out of his inside pocket, handing it over to her. "We got a request to investigate, the old man calling in a favor if you like, and we came down, firstly just to talk to the old lady to see if there was anything in the story. Wiggo here thought it was just a load of old bollocks."

"And what does he think now?" the policewoman said sarcastically.

"The same as you, I'd guess," Duffield said calmly. "Something is definitely the fuck going on around here. I suggest we stop dancing around each other and work together to figure out what."

The policewoman looked like she was about to argue some more, then seemed to come to a decision. She quickly read old George's letter.

"I've heard this story," she said, giving it back to him. "There's nothing new here for me."

"Apart from the fact that the old lady appears to be telling the truth. The dog is real, it's here, and Wiggo saw it," Duffield replied. "And trust me, he's not a man given to flights of fancy."

'Well, not unless there's a woman involved," Wiggo said, then went quiet when he saw Duffield's mood.

Duffield waited for the woman to make her mind up; he knew it could go either way. She could dismiss them entirely, or she could ask for all the help she could get. With all that was going on outside the bar at that moment, he hoped she'd make the right choice.

"Who the hell are you guys?" she said. "You're certainly not regular army."

"We're the guys who get called in when any strange beasties show up."

"So, like the X-Files?" Dave, the barman, said.

"Aye," Wiggo replied. "And I'm the pretty one."

"Look, I don't have time to be farting around here," Jenny said. "The village is in trouble enough as it is, what with the flooding. And that's going to get worse if this rain doesn't stop. I need to get the people out of here. But the phones are out."

"And so is the internet," Dave added. He'd moved behind the bar and was checking the credit card reader beside the till.

"I can maybe help with that," Duffield said. He reached into his inside pocket and came up with the satphone. He checked and there was a strong signal. He passed the phone to the policewoman.

"Should connect with any number you want to contact," he said.

"Thanks," she said, and managed a thin smile. "Sorry if I came on a bit strong."

"Understandable," Duffield replied, but she'd already walked away, and was punching out a number.

"What now, boss?" Wilkins said while helping himself to a swig from the whisky bottle.

"We need to find out more about whatever it was Wiggo saw," Duffield replied. "But these folks need help too. Let's see what her phone call brings."

Wilkins passed round some smokes. Wiggo nearly choked on his first puff, but determination and bloody mindedness pushed him through it. He looked up at Wilkins.

"Was it as bad as she said? The big man, I mean?"

"Worse, Sarge. You don't want to know."

"I owe him a couple of pints, and more," Wiggo said. "Somebody is going to be paying that debt."

It looked like the policewoman had got through to someone, and was in animated conversation.

Duffield turned his attention back to Wiggo. The sergeant looked exhausted.

"Get yourself upstairs and into dry clothes, Wiggo. Then get some rest. And that's an order I expect to be obeyed."

Wiggo saluted with the whisky bottle.

"Okay if I take this pal with me, boss?"

"Just don't get plastered. We might yet be needing your services tonight."

Wilkins helped Wiggo out of his chair. The sergeant's legs almost gave way under him, but he kept a tight grip on the bottle and didn't spill a drop, so Duffield reckoned he was going to be okay after some lie-down time. Wiggo proved it by turning back at the door.

"Boss? Thanks for the lift. I won't forget it."

Jenny got off the phone and walked over to hand it back to Duffield.

"They took some persuading; things are bad all over and they're stretched thin. But they're going to try and get some help to us. They've asked me to gather everyone in one place, so I said the church hall up at the vicarage. It's got the advantage of being the highest point too. Will you help me get everybody there?"

"Just tell me what you need."

- HARRY -

Harry was in trouble.

He'd tried to skirt the growing inflow of water at the rugby ground by heading out onto the low field below the cemetery but had been cut off, both front and back, by a sudden influx and had been forced north and west to the only high ground available, a roughly circular wooded copse over an ancient burial mound that sat alone in an otherwise flat area. The mound had been overgrown for as long as anyone could remember and was known locally as Old Tom's Tit.

With the water at his heels he clambered over the remains of an ancient dry-stone wall, climbed through gnarled trees and bramble bushes using the shotgun as a pole to clear the way, and finally stood at the highest point, sodden through, teeth chattering and as tired as he'd ever felt, watching as the waters rose steadily around the mound.

A foaming torrent now blocked his egress in every direction. Looking north and east through the trees, the cemetery and the lights of the vicarage above it flickered in the rain, only four hundred yards away but might as well be four hundred miles.

Well, this is fucking marvelous, isn't it? he muttered under his breath.

At least he was mostly out of the rain and wind, protected by a jacket of foliage, but there was still a steady flow of water falling from the branches above and finding its way down between his clothes and his neck. He stood ankle-deep in a pool of water gathering in the concave hollow area at the top of the mound, his feet feeling like blocks of ice, the cold already seeping upwards past his knees.

I can't stay here. It'll be the death of me.

Even as he thought it he was remembering the last time he'd stood in this spot.

It had been thirty years ago, twelve years old, heart pounding, pushing through the brambles on a dare and praying that the Black Shuck stories were really, as his dad said, 'just a load of old bollocks' for Old Tom's Tit was known by everyone to be the spot where the hound lay sleeping, and it didn't do to wake him up.

All he'd got for his trouble that time had been legs scratched to buggery by the bramble thorns and a general feeling that he shouldn't have been there. That same feeling came back in force now; his hindbrain told him to run, as fast as possible, just be anywhere but here. His rational mind considered the ramifications of that course of action; almost certain drowning in the torrent that surrounded him. As of now self-preservation was winning, but the feeling of wrongness got stronger by the second. He didn't think he was alone on the mound, and no amount of rationality would dispel that thought.

66

The water continued to rise. It was soon going to be a moot point; the flood was obviously going to be the winner of any argument here tonight. But still he couldn't talk himself into leaving a spot of comparative safety; he'd seen what the force of water had done to his house; his body didn't stand a chance.

He still couldn't shake the feeling that he was being watched. He drew his gaze away from the rising water and looked around the top of the mound. The foliage blocked much of the view, and looking down only showed him a growing puddle and scattered blocks of worked stone where the old mound had fallen in on itself in partial ruin. The water appeared to be running away below him, disappearing somewhere inside the mound itself.

Harry took a step back. The water ran ever faster, the stones under foot shifting in their place under the pressure of water. He stepped to one side, looking for firmer footing, but found exactly the opposite; the ground slid away under his feet. He threw himself backwards onto his backside as the mound gave way below him, scrambling for purchase as a black hole opened up just beyond his feet.

He had to use the shotgun, barrel downwards, to push himself away, then use it again like a support to help him stand. Once he felt steady he saw to his dismay that the barrels were both clogged tight with wet mud; there was no chance of using the weapon if it was needed.

And it was most definitely needed.

Something came up slowly out of the darkness below. At first Harry wasn't quite sure what he was looking at, his sight obscured by dripping water and general gloom, but he smelled it all right; wet dog and old meat, and when it snarled he heard it, clear even above the wail of the storm and lash of rain on leaves. He wiped his eyes on a wet sleeve and looked up, straight into a pair of blood-red eyes set almost a foot apart in a huge, black, shaggy head. Slavering jaws opened showing a lolling, red tongue and rows of long, yellowing teeth.

Harry didn't give himself time to think. He raised the shotgun, aimed between the red eyes, remembered the plugged barrels, and pulled the triggers anyway.

The blast deafened him, the recoil threw him back, into and through the foliage to totter, precariously, right above the roaring torrent. He tried to use the shotgun again as a walking stick to help him regain his balance but it snagged on a rock, and was immediately tugged out of his hands by the force of water. He looked back over his shoulder, saw a huge shadowy figure pull itself up out of the tumbling ruins of the mound, saw red eyes turn to gaze in his direction, and decided the water was a preferable option after all.

He dived in head first and let it take him where it willed.

- WIGGO -

Wiggo lay on top of his bed, eyeing the whisky bottle that sat on the bedside cabinet, but he'd already had two large stiffeners; if he got into it again now he might not stop until the bottle was empty.

And I promised the boss.

The very fact that he was thinking of Duffield in those terms also told him something else; he had now made peace with the arrival of the lieutenant on the scene.

All it took was for me to lose a man.

The memory of the big lad getting taken wasn't one he was going to be forgetting for a while, if ever, but he forced it down and away, filing it with the others that waited there for lonely nights, alone, in the dark, just him and a bottle. There were a lot of others.

But the filing system was one that could, in the light, be thankfully locked, a trick his old sergeant had taught him when Wiggo was just a private himself, and one that had stood him in good stead in the years since. But in order for the trick to work properly, he needed something else on his mind, and all there was here to think about was the bottle, and its promise of oblivion. He switched on the room's TV and got nothing but static; the signal had obviously gone the same way as the internet.

Enforced bed rest wasn't the answer… while lying down all he heard was the sounds of the storm, and that only served to remind him of the wall of sandbags and the events after their collapse. The bottle, however enticing it was, wasn't the answer either. He gave in, got up and stretched, feeling a dull ache throughout his upper torso, another memory of the time spent holding onto a tree for grim death and of the thing that came out of the dark.

He shivered, not from the cold. At least he was warm now, and dry in a change of clothing, but the memory of that cold wet time in the flood was another that he was sure would be with him for a long time to come.

Grim death.

Just the phrase threatened to bring the memories back again. He went to his gear and retrieved a pack of cigarettes. There was a lovely big sign on the back of the door telling him there was to be no smoking in the room. He'd liked the big barman, so, to spare his sensitivities, Wiggo went to the window and slid the sash frame open. He immediately let some of the storm in, but it was kid's stuff compared to what he'd been lost in earlier and no real impediment to an addicted smoker in search of a fix. Wiggo cupped his smoke against the wind, lit up and stared out over the small village square.

There wasn't much to see. The squad's 4WD was still parked at the curb by the front door, but there was no other traffic, and nowt to see but lashing rain, nothing to hear but the howl of the wind. Then the smell came to him; at first he thought it was still his memory playing tricks, but when he took the cigarette from his mouth he could still smell it; wet hair and bad meat.

The fucker's here. And close.

Wiggo flicked his smoke out the window into the night and headed for his gear.

Two minutes later he was back down in the public bar, zipping up his waterproofs and ensuring his handgun was snug in the holster at his right hip.

Without a qualm he went back out into the storm.

I owe the big man that much.

The storm immediately hit him full in the face. He turned his head against it and looked over the square. There was still nothing to see, but the smell, although fainter, was still there.

"Show yourself, fucker, if you've got the balls for it."

Wiggo knew his voice wouldn't carry far in the wind, but he also had a strong feeling that the beast would hear him anyway, just as he was already sure that this was indeed more in the way of one of Seton's bogles than in any physical beast. He reached for his pistol, knowing it might be useless but enjoying the weight and heft of it in his hand. He was about to call out again when another sound carried through the storm, the quick double retort that he knew only meant one thing.

Shotgun!

He turned towards the sound and headed as fast as he could manage, down the hill, making for the flood.

He couldn't see anything at first when he reached the water's edge, just foaming, roiling water. Then a head bobbed above the surface some ten yards out, a man gasping for air, just once before he went under again. Wiggo didn't stop to think. He dropped his gun on the grass and launched himself into the flood, feeling it immediately tug and pull at him as if he was unfinished business from the last time.

"No one else dies tonight," Wiggo said grimly. "Not on my watch."

He tried to gauge where the man might be, waded out to that spot and, for the first time that night, got lucky; the man bobbed up just two feet away from him. Wiggo planted his feet against the current as well as he could and put out a hand. The man surfaced, saw Wiggo, and reached for him. Their fingers touched.

"Got you, you lucky fucker," Wiggo said, grabbed the man by the wrist and, with no little effort, reeled him in. That was the easy bit; now he had to get them both back to shore. The current was tugging even harder at him now, not wanting to lose its prize.

"Need some help here," Wiggo shouted in the man's face. His catch looked half-drowned, but managed a nod and finally they both got their feet under them and started to plough towards shore, the current threatening to dislodge them at every step.

The flood made one final attempt, raising Wiggo's feet off the bottom.

"Not tonight, Josephine," Wiggo said, and lunged for the shore, dragging the man with him. With one last effort he threw them both out of the water to land with a splash in the sodden grass on the waterline. He rolled to his feet, took the man's arms and dragged him away as far as he could manage until his strength left him in a rush and he collapsed beside the gasping man.

And then he got lucky again, for on rolling over he saw his gun, lying just yards away on the grass. It took what little strength he had left to crawl over to it. He clutched it to his chest, rolled onto his back and fired four shots into the air, two by two.

The rescued man still lay on his back, spluttering.

"Hold on mate, the cavalry's coming," Wiggo shouted, then a wave of tiredness washed over him and blackness called again.

He went to it willingly.

- DUFFIELD -

"You're doing this just to piss me off, aren't you?" Duffield said, looking down to where Wiggo lay on the wet grass.

They'd been trying to persuade two recalcitrant pensioners out of their cottage when they heard, first a shotgun going off then, minutes later when they were already out on the road, four quick pistol shots. It only took them a couple of minutes after that to find the two prone bodies on the grass near the edge of the flooded area. Duffield had bent, checked, and found a pulse. Concern was giving way to irritation, then just as quickly, relief.

Wiggo's eyes opened and the sergeant managed a thin smile.

"Just testing out the new man," the sergeant said.

"Aye? Well, don't be making a habit of it, Wiggo. I'm testy enough as it is right now. And don't think I'm carrying you back up that fucking hill again. Get to your feet, soldier. That's a fucking order, in case you didn't notice."

He put out a hand, was pleased to see that Wiggo had the energy to take it, and dragged the sergeant upright.

"That's two you owe me."

"We're keeping tabs now?"

"Fucking right we are. Want to tell me what you were doing fucking about in the water again, Sarge?"

Wiggo didn't get time to answer; the rescued man beat him to it. He was being helped up by the policewoman and her husband.

"He was saving my fucking life, that's what he was fucking doing," he said wearily. "And right glad I am of it too. I thought Black Shuck had done for me for sure."

"The big dog? You've seen it?" Jenny said.

"Seen it, put two 12-bore cartridges in its head and didn't seem to slow it down much. I suggest we get the fuck to somewhere safe as soon as we can before it gets curious."

There were obviously stories to be told, but there was no sense in standing in a storm listening to them. Duffield motioned to the rescued man.

"Can you walk?"

The man nodded, and Dave replied.

"We've got him. You see to your man, we'll see to ours."

"Back to the bar it is then," Duffield said.

"Best offer I've had all week," Wiggo said. "But I could use a shoulder to lean on, boss? I'm fair wabbit."

Ten minutes later they were all back in the bar. Wiggo and the rescued man... Harry the policewoman had called him... were getting into dry clothes. Wilko and Mac donated their spare sets, neither of which were perfect fits but at least the two half-drowned men were now dry again, if not exactly comfortable.

Dave wheeled out whisky on the house again.

"This is costing me a small fortune," he said wryly.

"I'll see you get the money back," Duffield said. "I'll put an expenses claim in with the Ministry."

"Aye, good luck with that one, boss," Wiggo said.

The sergeant already had some color back in his cheeks and Harry, although bone tired, was taking to the Scotch well enough... a bit too well if truth be told.

I'll have to get his story now, before he gets pished.

"Tell me about the black dog," Duffield said, sitting down across the table.

The farmer looked first to the policewoman.

"It's okay, Harry. They're here to help," Jenny said.

"I'm not sure anybody can," Harry said quietly. "But I'll tell you. It started when the floodwater reached the farmhouse... "

"The farmhouse?" Dave said. "But that's eight feet above high water."

"It was ten feet above," Harry replied. "It isn't now. But let me tell it. I don't have the energy to be stopping and starting all the time."

They got the farmer's story out of him in fits and starts between more pauses for whisky and when it was done he slumped in the chair, head in his hands.

"Lost the farm, lost my flock... even lost the fucking shotgun. What the fuck am I going to do now?"

Nobody had an answer for him.

Duffield nodded to Wiggo in the silence that followed. The sergeant's story didn't take nearly as long, and then Duffield brought Wiggo up to speed on what else was going on.

"While you were out disobeying orders, we've been rounding up folks and getting them to the Church Hall. Jenny tells me Harry's the last of them. A couple of the auld folk were hard to persuade, and Eleanor up at the vicarage is adamant she's staying put, even though her home-help is among those now in the hall. We've got everybody else from the village ready and waiting for when the choppers arrive, a couple of dozen of them, auld folks mainly."

Wiggo pointed out at the weather; the wind had got up a notch if anything, and the rain lashed hard against the windows.

"There won't be anyone flying in this shite. Ye ken that, boss."

"Aye. But at least we're ready for when they are. Best we can do right now."

"So when do we start doing what we came here to do?"

"I was hoping you wouldn't ask me that."

"I was hoping you'd say something before I asked."

"Touche, Mr. Pussycat," Duffield replied in an outrageous French accent and got a wide grin in reply from Wiggo. "We'd better get started on hunting it down. You strong enough for a wee walk?"

"Aye, it's a fine night for it," Wiggo replied.

"I'd start somewhere down near Old Tom's Tit," Harry said, reaching for a whisky bottle that was getting emptier by the minute. "That's where the bulk of sightings over the years have been. You won't get close because of the flood, but maybe that's not a bad thing."

Harry went back to sucking on the bottle as Duffield turned to the policewoman.

"You'll watch him?"

"Yes. We'll take him up to be with the others in the Church Hall. That's where anybody who comes will be expecting to find us. After we've got him there Dave and I will do a last check to make sure we haven't missed anybody. Then we'll head back to the hall too."

"And that's where we'll find you. We'll do a sweep searching for the beastie, see if we can get to the bottom of this."

"There is no bottom," Harry muttered drunkenly. "Just a tunnel leading all the way to Hell."

Duffield checked his watch while everyone was getting into their waterproofs and was surprised to find it wasn't even ten o' clock yet; it felt like the day had been going on forever.

And it's not done with us yet. I feel it in my bones.

But Wiggo had been right; it was past time they got about doing what they'd been sent to do. The old lady's story rang true, and he couldn't deny both Wiggo and Harry's stories. There was a beast here to be rid of; maybe not the kind of beastie he'd expected to be fighting when he took the job on, but a beastie nevertheless.

Time to get to it.

He made sure everybody was ready and led the squad back out into the storm.

- HARRY -

Harry got soaked through again on the short walk from the pub up to the Church Hall but he hardly noticed. A deep tiredness had settled in his bones, and what with that and the whisky he was more than half asleep; Dave the barman almost carried him up the short stretch of road.

The cold rain and wind revived him a little, and the sight of almost everyone he knew huddled in the confines of the small hall forced his addled mind to return, if only for a moment, to the reality of the situation. That reality rushed in closer when Dave put him down in a seat… next to old Bob Brown, the blowhard from the pub. If he'd had the energy Harry might have moved, but his legs had stopped obeying him, and old Bob had a captive audience. It quickly became clear he meant to take full advantage of it.

"Well this is a pretty pass, isn't it," Bob started in immediately. "I told you all that everything was going to go to shit, didn't I tell you? Just this very afternoon I told you, and look where we are now. We'll be lucky if we've got any homes left to go back to. All this and Black Shuck on the prowl too. It's that old bitch in the vicarage's fault, I'm sure of it. Why else would they send a black ops team to see her? I wouldn't be surprised if she got quietly disappeared, although somebody should have done the necessary to that family fucking years ago; haven't I been saying that too? And another thing..."

"Bob," Harry said wearily, "I've had a fuck of a bad day, and I don't need any of your fucking bullshit. Give it a fucking rest would you for once in your miserable life?"

"You think you're the only one who's had a bad day? My kitchen floor's ruined."

Harry laughed bitterly.

"Fuck your kitchen floor. My farm is gone. My whole fucking life is gone down the river, probably somewhere near Colchester by now, my flock has gone, your Black Shuck tried to bite me in the arse and I nearly drowned. You want to compare days? You want to whine some more about your fucking kitchen floor? Fuck off before you get the slap you've deserved for too many years."

Bob looked like he might reply but he must have seen something in Harry's eyes. He backed off, hands raised.

"Hey. I was just talking."

"And there's your fucking problem right there. You never stop just talking."

Harry hoisted the whisky bottle, pointedly refused to offer it to the older man, and downed what was left of it in two swift gulps. It hit him like a train and he was down for the count again seconds later.

It isn't blissful oblivion that waits for him; it's a nightmare. He is back on Old Tom's Tit. Cold water drips from above, the ground shifts under his feet even as wind whistles through thrashing branches. He smells it, wet dog, meat gone bad, red eyes glowing as it comes up out of the hole. He turns, tries to run, but the tiredness has him now and his legs refuse the order. All he can do is stand and watch as the hound comes for him, licking its lips with a tongue like a slab of stone. A scream won't come, caught deep in his throat, no more than a tired whisper. When he raises his hands there is no welcome weight of a shotgun there, just wet fingers grasping feebly at the air, warm now where the beast breathes on them.

It speaks, low, gravelly, bestial yet human all at the same time.

"Are ye a herdsman yet, or are ye done?"

The ground below him collapses completely and Harry falls, a long time, lost in darkness, bobbing like a balloon finding its way to earth. Finally, after an age, his feet hit more solid ground, or rather flooring, cold stone, damp flagstones, green moss and the smell, even stronger now, wet dog, bad meat.

"Are ye a herdsman yet?" it says, breath warm in his ear as, slowly, Harry's eyes adjust to the gloom.

He stands in a slaughterhouse to match that in his barn, but these bones, although also strewn far and wide inside the chamber, are old, grey and bloodless. They are also, clearly, not sheep; three grinning skulls show all too human smiles of yellowed and broken teeth.

"Ye hae your herd, and I hae mine," the voice says. "I will hae mine again. Are ye a herdsman yet?"

"What the fuck do you want of me?" Harry screamed.

Harry woke, blearily, to someone shaking his shoulder. He looked up into Bob the blowhard's face.

"What the fuck is it now?" Harry said.

"Nowt to do with me, lad," Bob said, suddenly backing off as if afraid. "I was just wondering why you were screaming."

Harry looked around the room. Almost everyone was looking at him. It struck him again that most of the people he'd spent any time with in his lifetime were gathered here, congregated in one place. One word had come up with him out of the dream.

Herded.

He got a chill in his bones, and this time he was pretty sure it was nothing to do with the rain.

- WIGGO -

Wiggo wasn't as knackered as he should be, a combination of the whisky and adrenaline that he knew from experience was going to lead to a fuck of a crash sometime sooner rather than later. But for now he felt just fine and wouldn't be anywhere else for all the tea in China. Despite the rigours of this current job... or maybe even because of them... Wiggo was coming to realise he was exactly where he wanted to be; with a squad of like-minded lads, fighting the good fight. A promotion would be nice and all that, but he'd be having to cope with a fuckload of admin and administrative headaches as a staff sergeant that he just didn't get exposed to out in the field. Sure, the extra money would come in handy.

But I spend enough on fags and booze as it is. What am I going to do with the rest? Start up a fucking pension fund?

With wind roaring in his ears and rain lashing in his face, Wiggo allowed himself a wide grin.

"What the fuck are you so happy about, Sarge?" Duffield asked.

"Just looking on the bright side of life, boss," Wiggo said. "And glad not to be deid."

"Just see you stay that way," Duffleld replied with a grin of his own. "I'd miss you."

"I bet you say that to all the girls."

The rain showed no signs of slacking, and they only got a touch of respite when they turned a corner and had it mostly drumming into them from behind rather than a full frontal assault. Wiggo could scarcely see ten yards in any direction. The ground underfoot was sodden through and they splashed up water with every step.

"Oh I do like to be beside the seaside," Wiggo sang, loudly, and after a laugh they all joined in. They got as far as the first chorus before Duffield called a stop, one hand raised in a fist.

They stood in silence, just the roar of the wind in their ears.

"Thought I heard something," Duffield said. "Like a howl, but it might just have been the wind."

"Probably Mac's singing," Wiggo said. "I thought somebody was strangling a cat."

Duffield called for silence again, but again there were only the sounds of the storm. They moved off seconds later, the lieutenant moving more cautiously and the others following his lead.

Wilkins and Wiggo walked side by side down a narrow, cobbled alleyway that led between a pair of houses heading for the flat ground of what had been the playing fields. The alley was serving as a funnel for the rain, and washes of water ran down the walls on either side and ran in a runnel at their feet.

"So what was it like, Sarge?" Wilkins said. "This big black dug."

"It looked like a fucking big black dug," Wiggo said, remembering. "No, actually, more like a fucking black bear. Did I say it was big? Like, I mean, it was fucking huge." He held out a hand at shoulder height. "This big, maybe bigger, and it smelt like it had shat itself then rolled in it. Ye're no' going to be mistaking it for anything else."

They came out of the alleyway and again walked into the full force of the storm. Wind tugged at them and rain lashed against their waterproofs. The lieutenant had to pull them all together, heads close, to make himself heard.

"The last sighting was by that lad, Harry, somewhere near here," he said. "Yon mound he called 'Old Tom's Tit' is over to the north. So we'll head that way first and have a shufti. Heads up and eyes open, lads, and if you see it, shoot first and ask questions later."

He didn't mention the fact that Harry had, supposedly, put two shotgun cartridges in the thing; he didn't have to. And Wiggo thought it wouldn't make much difference anyway.

"It's a fucking bogle," he thought, and didn't say. "It's brains we'll be needing, not pistols."

But this was the young lieutenant's show, and his first one at that. Wiggo now owed him time to either get the job done, or to fuck it up royally. Either way, he'd have the lad's back for the duration.

It became immediately obvious that the flood water had risen even further since Wiggo and Harry's escapades earlier. The playing fields had long since been filled and the spate lapped up against the low wall at the foot of the cemetery that marked the boundary of the old village. The mound Harry had referred to was somewhere out in the gloom across the water, a couple of hundred yards away but hidden from sight in the storm and with a roaring torrent between it and the squad; it might as well have been on the moon.

The lieutenant led them a bit further north alongside the cemetery wall, and kept looking up to his right towards the church, then left in the direction of the mound across the water, as if checking the line of sight. Wiggo was about to step up and ask a question when he smelled it again, the unmistakable tang of wet dog, bad meat and shite.

He grabbed the lieutenant by the shoulder and shouted in his ear.

"It's here. It's close."

The lieutenant wasted no time. He pulled the four men together, back to back. They unholstered their pistols. Wiggo ended up looking east, up the hill across the cemetery to where the lights of the vicarage and the church hall flickered and glimmered through the rain. He smelled it again before he saw it, little more than a darker shadow moving among the old graves, some ten yards away where the ground started to rise upwards towards the church and vicarage. It kept close to the ground, head down, moving parallel to the wall where the soldiers stood. He couldn't see its eyes, would hardly have known it was there but for the smell, which came stronger again in the wind.

Wiggo raised his pistol. As if it had seen him and knew his intent, the blackness merged deeper into the shadows under the trees, not leaving him a clear shot.

"I see you, you bastard," Wiggo muttered and kept his pistol raised.

The next time he saw it, it was five yards higher up the slope, a sleek black shadow still hugging the ground as it moved among the stones. And now it really did take note of him. Fiery red eyes turned to look straight at Wiggo. They flared, as if someone had blown on hot coals.

"Come on then, you wanker," Wiggo said. "Let's see what you've got."

The beast didn't react, but moved away again and continued to weave through the stones, getting farther away as it tacked slowly up the hill.

"Bugger," Wiggo muttered and lowered his pistol before turning to the others. "I couldn't get a clear shot. It's away up to the village."

The lights above them flickered and the beast howled into the storm. The black shadow leapt away upwards, and suddenly Wiggo's heart sank as he remembered where the town's people were gathered.

It's headed straight for the Church Hall.

And they don't know it's coming.

- HARRY -

The Church Hall was as quiet as Harry had ever seen it. On a good day it would have been full of noise and good cheer; pensioners' coffee mornings, local talent shows, bingo nights, even town council meetings all brought with them conversation and often laughter. But this wasn't a good day. People sat quiet even when huddled together in family groups, and any voices were low and subdued, whispers that ran through the hall like church mice in search of food scraps. Harry knew almost everybody present, and had even nodded to the incomer couple he'd seen in the bar earlier. Old Bob was keeping Harry at arm's length, which was fine by him. The whisky bottle lay cradled in his arms like a child. It was empty now, and any warmth he'd got from it was fading fast as a chill he couldn't shift settled in his bones.

Harry dozed, dipping in and out of a sleep he didn't want to fall completely into in case he was tossed into another nightmare.

Instead, the nightmare came to him.

It started with a thumping, like a softly beaten drum, so quiet at first that he thought it was little more than the pounding of blood in his ears. He tried to ignore it, then saw that he wasn't the only one who had taken note.

Somebody shouted from behind Harry.

"Get that bloody door! There's some poor sod stuck out there in the rain."

Old Bob stood up from his chair and headed towards the door. The drumming immediately became an insistent pounding, shaking the door in its frame. Harry knew with absolute certainty what was outside. He stood, too quickly, knocking over his chair, the crash causing everybody in the hall to go quiet and look in his direction. Harry's full attention was on the doorway as old Bob stepped up closer to it.

"Stay away from there," Harry shouted. "Get back. It's not safe."

He tried to move forward but his legs refused the order.

Old Bob shouted back at him.

"You're the one that's not safe, sitting there screaming to yourself. You don't get to tell me what to do, you useless fucker," the older man said. "There's a poor soul still out in the rain that needs letting in. Some of us still have good Christian thoughts in our heads, even if you don't."

The door banged even harder as Bob reached for the handle.

"This has got nothing to do with Christianity," Harry said.

"Exactly what I'd expect from a godless bastard like you," Bob said, then turned back to the door. "Hold your horses, I'm coming."

They were to be the last words he ever uttered.

He turned the handle. The door flew open with a clatter like a gunshot, banging hard enough against the wall to take out a dinner plate-sized chunk of plaster. The door-frame filled with the head and shoulders of the great black hound. Its eyes blazed as it looked around the hall then fixed their gaze where old Bob stood, riveted to the spot, a slack jawed gape of astonishment on his face and a dribble of piss running between his trouser leg and his shoes.

"Bob," Harry said, trying to keep his voice soft and low. "Come back here. Come to me."

Bob either didn't hear him, or couldn't move even if he wanted to. The beast took a step forward, its gaze still fixed on the man. It raised its head and howled, a wail that echoed for long seconds in the hall and set off an immediate commotion.

Panic spread quickly. Chairs were overturned, bodies fell over each other and screams rose in the wind. Harry stood his ground, bearing witness to what he feared was about to happen.

The beast lunged forward, its jaws opened, and closed again around old Bob's waist, almost biting him in half. Blood spattered across the doorway and the surrounding wall, some of it even reaching the roof, spraying across the overhead light and casting a pink-red tinge over everything below. The head lowered Bob's body to the floor. The dog put one great paw on the man's chest, closed its jaws on his head, and ripped it off the body as easily as twisting a flower off a stem.

Harry realised he still had the whisky bottle in his hand. Without considering the consequences he raised and threw it in one smooth motion, hitting the beast full on the snout. The bottle, miraculously, didn't break and bounced away across the floor.

Harry smelled it again, wet hair and dead meat. The black dog raised its head. It looked like it was smiling as it looked straight at him. It snarled and took a step forward.

Harry threw himself backwards, tripping over his tumbled chair before rolling over, hitting the floor hard. All around him people were still fleeing in panic, heading for the rear of the hall, as far from the hound as they could get. Harry got kicked on the side of the head, rolled again, sprawling on the floor, catching fleeting images of unfolding carnage.

The hound leapt out of the doorway, an impossible bound that took it all the way across the hall to land among the terrified townsfolk who were gathered in a group trying to open the rear door. It scattered them like bowling pins across the floor, sending them banging onto walls and windows even as its jaws worked like an industrial crusher on their fat, muscle and bones. Red spray and screams, all too brief screams, filled the hall, while Harry was still trying to push himself upright.

By the time he got unsteadily to his feet it was almost all over.

It was the scene in his barn played over again, only this time with people rather than sheep; parts and bones and blood and guts strewn in a wide swathe across the floor, walls and ceiling of the hall, the air filled with the stench of shit and blood, the only sound the crunch of teeth on bone as the beast chowed down on the last remnants of someone's grandmother. None of the bodies moved; probably a blessing given how torn and mutilated they were.

Harry took a single step, towards the beast rather than away from it. Its head came up, blood and gore hanging in a ropy drool from its jaws. It looked him in the eye and smiled. He heard it inside his head.

"Are ye a herdsman yet?"

"Rather a herdsman than a butcher," Harry muttered. "What do you want from me?"

"An answer," the voice replied.

Before Harry had time to digest that he heard voices at his back, then a shouted command.

"Get down."

He threw himself to the floor as gunfire erupted above his head.

- DUFFIELD -

The squad arrived at the Church Hall out of breath and soaked through, having run up the hill at full pelt in the storm. Duffield had been hoping all the way; hoping that he'd get a clear shot at the thing, hoping that the hall was secure enough to keep the beast out, hoping that it would just give up and fuck off. But they were all false hopes and he already knew they were too late as soon as he saw the open door.

His heart sank with his first look at the charnel-house carnage that surrounded the creature at the far end of the hall. It dominated the whole room, a huge black semi-shadowy figure, almost a silhouette against the white plastered walls of the hall, rampaging among the bodies, most thankfully already dead, biting down on limbs and necks and stomping on rib cages, the sound of bones breaking like gunfire in the enclosed space.

Duffield raised his pistol, but the local, Harry, was directly in line of a head shot.

"Get down!" he shouted and thankfully the man obliged. The rest of the squad quickly lined up at his side as they pumped round after round into the beast.

The black dog continued to rampage among the bodies of the victims. It was like shooting a cloud; none of their bullets had any effect; the beast simply stood there, stomping amid a pool of blood and gore as if dancing, its tongue lolling and drool running from the corners of its mouth. The only sign that it took note of the shooting was the too-red eyes, which flashed at each pistol shot.

Despite the lack of effect, Duffield didn't hesitate, couldn't afford to. He came up empty and had to reload. In the same movement he stepped forward closer to the hound, then closer still when he was able to fire again. The squad came forward with him. Wiggo shouted at his side.

"Why won't you just fucking die?"

All four of the squad strode further forward, still firing; Harry had the good sense to roll aside to let them pass unheeded. But still the volley fire had no discernible effect. Wiggo shouted again.

"Just fuck off, will ye? Ya fuckin' bogle bastard."

The hound licked its lips and seemed to smile. It leaned back, weight shifting to its hind quarters, then launched itself into a leap at the largest window. It took out the window, the frame and some of the surrounding masonry as it went through; for a second Duffield had wondered whether it might just pass like water through a colander.

It's physical enough, that's for sure.

Silence fell in the hall even as the gunshots continued to ring in Duffield's ears. He stepped up to the window, got a blast of rain in his face for his trouble, and looked out. There was nothing to see but darkness and the thrashing of trees in the wind.

Wiggo stepped up at his side.

"Do bogles generally do shite like that, Sarge?" Duffield asked.

"Don't ask me, boss. I just work here," Wiggo replied.

Duffield went to stand amid the bloody carnage. There had been upwards of two dozen people here; he knew because he'd brought some of them in himself, mainly old and infirm. The beast had shown no mercy for age or circumstance and had slaughtered them all indiscriminately. All that was left was gore and body parts and a stench of death that he knew would linger with him long after he had left this place.

Wilkins drew their attention to the wall at the rear end of the hall; the plasterwork was riddled with bullet holes.

"We can't all be crap shots," Duffield said. "You're saying they all went right through it."

"I'm saying nowt, boss," Wilkins replied. "Except that a good stiff drink seems to be in order."

A scream, high and long, rose up from the front of the hall; the policewoman, Jenny, and her husband had returned. Duffield had to catch her in his arms as she ran full pelt the length of the floor towards them, still screaming. She fought like a devil, squirming in his arms, screaming in his face.

"Let me go. I need to see."

"No, lass. You don't want to see this. Trust me."

"What happened?" she shouted through a flood of sudden tears. "What the fuck happened here? Why didn't you stop it?"

It was Harry who eventually answered.

"Black Shuck happened. He came for his flock. Same as it ever was."

Despite her protestations Duffield wouldn't allow Jenny to have anything to do with the cleanup.

"You knew these people. They're your friends. This is a pain you don't need. Trust me on this... I've been there."

She buried her head in his chest, just for a second, then turned away, pointedly keeping her eyes on her husband.

Duffield turned to Dave.

"Take her to the bar. Get a drink inside the both of you. We'll meet you there when we've finished here."

Dave looked like he was ready to throw up...and Duffield wouldn't have blamed him in the slightest; the thought of what was in the squad's immediate future filled him with a deep seated dread, and for the first time he was glad he hadn't had too much to eat so far that day. He'd been on clean-up crews before, even led teams cleaning up the aftermath of some of the squad's previous missions. But this would be a first; the people here should have been under his protection, his responsibility. Now this mess was all that was left of them, and he'd have to clean it without ever getting the chance to say sorry. If this was the burden of command, right now he wasn't sure he wanted it.

The barman and Jenny left... she never looked back. Duffield gave them time to get out of earshot then looked around, wondering where to start.

Harry, to everyone's surprise, turned out to be the practical one.

"My old mum was the cleaner here when I was a lad, and things haven't changed any. I know where everything's kept."

He showed them the janitor's closet off to one side of the hall, where they found what they needed in bin bags, mops, bleach and buckets.

"I know this isn't what you want to be doing right now, lads," he said. "It's not what I had in mind for the night either. But let's just grit our teeth and get this done. I'll stand for a couple of rounds once we get things squared up."

Harry surprised him again by volunteering his help.

"I know these folks... it's the least I can do."

Young MacIntosh looked a bit green about the gills at the prospect, but Duffield couldn't really hold it against him.

"You watch the window and door, lad, and shout if the fucker shows up again. We'll deal with this."

Then it couldn't be put off any longer. They got down to the hard part.

"This isn't right," Harry said while shovelling one particularly gruesome mess that had once been someone's torso into a bin liner. "They need to be buried. We need to do right by them. These were all good people."

Duffield patted the man on the shoulder.

"They will be honoured, I promise you that," he said softly. "But for now, all we can do is make sure they don't get any further defiled. We'll put them to rest once it's all over."

"This shit has been going on for centuries, man," Harry said quietly. "I don't think it's ever over... not around these parts."

In what little deference to the dead they were able to give, they had Harry's help and did their best to keep the remains alongside the appropriate parts, but it was an almost impossible task, and mopping up human beings with a broom and a bucket took its toll on all of them. There were several times Duffield was grateful again for the lack of food in his stomach, and even Wiggo, who Duffield thought was the most stoic of them all, had to step aside for a smoke break after finding a woman's head fully torn from her body, her eyes wide open but flat-blue, an accusing stare like a china doll.

It took half an hour, at the end of which time they had a small mound of black bin liner bags and a room that was almost clean if you could ignore the bullet holes and the pink stains on the floor and walls. Duffield couldn't.

He gave the lads a smoke break, went to stand by the front door, and took out the satphone. Captain Banks answered immediately, as if he'd been sitting waiting.

"It's all gone tits up here, Cap," Duffield said. "We've got multiple civilian casualties."

He heard Banks suck at his teeth even through the phone line.

"Is there a lid on it?" Banks asked.

"For now, aye, sir. As long as this storm lasts. But there's going to be a shitstorm somewhere down the line; the local law has been on the scene. And the thing that did it is still out there. It could get worse before it gets better. We need some backup; we're just fucking about in the dark here."

"Aye, well you're not going to get any in a hurry. Yon storm you said you're in the middle of is a beast. All flights are grounded, there's flooding all over the South-East and resources are stretched to breaking point. I'll do what I can for you, but it'll be a matter of hours at best, and probably not until morning. I'll keep the brass off your back as long as I can, but for now you're on your own. But that's why we pay you the big money," Banks said with a harsh laugh. "Trust your squad. They've been through worse. Give Wiggo his head if you need to. He's a good man in a tight spot."

"Yes, sir," Duffield said.

He thought the line had been cut for a second then Banks added, "And Joe? Trust yourself. You've got this."

- HARRY -

Harry stood in silence looking at the mound of black bin bags. Somewhere in there was old Bob the blowhard who would never bore a bar full of people ever again. Somewhere else was June Peabody, mother of one of the lads who had dared Harry to enter Old Tom's Tit all those years ago. Every bag represented someone he knew; even the two outsiders were there, the wrong place, wrong time folks now stuck in eternity alongside old Bob with no means of escape.

He was wool gathering; he knew it, but although he was standing once again his legs were refusing to take him anywhere. It felt like his brain was too full, overflowing with images, emotions, sights, sounds and, yes, smells even though bleach was now the dominant one.

The Scots' officer called out.

"Time we were all going."

Harry turned to him, and pointed at the black bags.

"We can't just leave them here. What if Shuck comes back for his supper?"

"I'm open to suggestions, man," the officer said. "But we can't bury them, not in this weather, and there's folks here still alive who need helping."

Harry looked at the bags and shook his head.

"They shouldn't just be left here waiting for the bin men. There's the church crypt? We could store them there; it's cold but it's dry, most of the time."

The officer paused; Harry saw the need in the younger man for action.

"Please," Harry said. "For pity's sake?"

The officer relented.

It was another job none of them relished, but Harry mucked in and did his bit and twenty minutes later they'd moved all the bags to the relative dryness and safety of the church. They didn't make it as far as the crypt, which was bolted and locked but at least here there were no bullet holes, no pink stains, and Harry could partially fool himself into thinking that the dead might get some kind of rest and respite from carnage and fear.

"Now can we get a drink, boss?" one of the soldiers said. "I'm fucking parched here."

"I think we could all use one," the officer said, and this time Harry could find nothing to disagree with and followed them out as they filtered from the church.

Walking in the storm while sober was a much more different experience than doing so when drunk. He preferred the drunk one. The rain was still pelting down, driven by a wind that threatened to toss him off his feet and up and away like Mary bloody Poppins. He was almost running, struggling to keep up with the soldiers who set a fast jogging pace. None of them spoke, and the weight of the dead they were leaving behind seemed to settle like sandbags on Harry's shoulders.

And now that they'd left the chapel, his thoughts turned away from the horror of the dead and back to his own personal terror, and to the way that Shuck had seemed to address him. Even now he felt those red eyes bore into him, as if tallying up his soul and finding it wanting. He heard again the gravelly voice, heard the questions being asked.

What the fuck does it want me for?

Now that he was sobering up he was afraid he was getting closer to finding an answer to that question.

Getting inside and out of the storm felt almost like coming home.

Dave had the bar open, and Jenny sat in one of the high stools, a large drink in hand. It looked like it wasn't her first. The barman didn't speak, just lined up a row of glasses and poured them all a stiff one. Harry tried not to seem too eager, but the squaddies were well ahead of him in any case. Wiggins lit up a cigarette and raised an eyebrow at the barman.

"Go ahead, lad," Dave said. "I doubt anybody's going to complain tonight."

The first drink settled Harry's jitters; a second threatened to bring them back. He put the glass down so that the others wouldn't see his hand shaking.

Jenny looked up from the bar, eyes red from tears.

"This isn't happening. Not here. Not in my town."

Dave put an arm round her, and looked to the soldiers.

"You came here for a reason. Maybe it's time you told us what that was."

The officer of the soldiers looked grim.

"At this point you know about as much about this mess as we do… probably more given that it's your town, your history, and we only just got here."

"But you're the army. Fucking do something," Jenny said bitterly.

"I'm working on it," Duffield replied.

"I'd suggest working faster," Dave said dryly as Jenny buried her face in his chest, sobbing bitterly.

"So what's the plan now, boss?" Wiggins said after an awkward minute when nobody spoke.

"We need some understanding of this thing…beastie…whatever the fuck it is. We need to find out why here, why now. We need to know what it wants."

Harry broke the silence that followed.

"Me. I think it wants me, although I couldn't for the life of me tell you why."

It took another stiff drink, then it all came out of him… the red eyes, the voice, the questions he couldn't answer. Nobody interrupted him until he was done.

"Herdsman?" the officer, Duffield, said. "It spoke to you to ask you that?"

Harry nodded.

"I know how it sounds, but I wasn't drunk... well, not totally."

"What does it mean?" Dave the barman asked.

Jenny answered; her voice was dull, her eyes watery again with fresh tears that had nothing to do with the booze.

"Eleanor will know. I've heard her use the word, more than once. And you know what she's like; there's more stories in her than she's ever let on. We should ask Eleanor."

"Could we get her to come here?" Duffield asked. "I'd like to have us all in one place."

Because that worked so well up at the Hall.

Harry thought it, but didn't say it. The soldiers were only trying to do their job; it wasn't their fault that nobody had told them what the job was in the first place.

"I'll go get her," Jenny said. She now looked more like the police officer, grim determination showing in her face, as if having something to do had reminded her of who she was at heart. Dave stood as she did.

"We'll both go."

"Not alone you won't," Duffield replied. "I'll come too. She knows me. Wiggo... you're in charge till I get back. Stay inside, and if it comes back..."

"I'll use harsh language," Wiggo replied. "And if that doesn't work I'll offer to lick its balls."

Jenny, Dave and Duffield left to fetch the old lady. Harry was left with the other three and the whisky but strangely it was no longer tempting him in the same way as before. Of course, he'd welcome the oblivion, but he wasn't sure now that was what waited for him in any self-induced stupor. He suspected that Shuck would be there, in his head, asking him the same questions to which he still had no answers.

Sergeant Wiggins brought over a bottle and sat beside him.

"Will ye take a drink with me, man," he said. "I think we both deserve more than one."

"Only if I can have a smoke too," Harry said, and returned Wiggins' smile in payment for a cigarette and another two fingers of the Scotch.

"Your beastie really spoke to you?" Wiggins asked after a time.

Harry nodded.

"Anything else you remember?"

"I've been trying to think. It all comes back to Old Tom's Tit. That's where the activity has always been centered. If it's answers you're after, that's where I'd start."

"Aye. The lieutenant's already got that in mind. But it's lost to us in the flood right now, a dead end. You got anything else?"

"I'm just a simple farmer, lad. Or at least, I was before today."

Wiggins clapped him on the shoulder.

"We'll get through this. You'll get it back."

But am I a Herdsman? Am I still a Herdsman?

The question continued to rattle around in the emptiness of his mind long after Wiggins moved away and left him alone with too many thoughts.

- DUFFIELD -

Duffield, Jenny and Dave sat damply perched on the edge of their seats around a fire that was on the verge of going out. Eleanor sat in an armchair like a queen of old holding court. She was wrapped in a long shawl that covered her from neck to ankles but did little to disguise just how thin and frail she was beneath it. Her voice was still strong though, and her eyes showed grim determination. She was proving to be intractable, even in the face of the downfall of the village. Nobody had told her of the carnage in the village hall, but she didn't need telling; she already knew something was afoot.

"I won't be leaving this house again. I'm staying right here," she said. "And you can't make me move... you shouldn't make me move. It'll just make things worse."

"Eleanor," Jenny said softly. "It's already as bad as it could get."

"No, it's not. Not yet," the old lady replied, and Duffield saw the fear in her eyes... fear and what looked like regret. "But I can't hold him much longer," she said, barely a whisper. "I've been doing it too long and I'm nearly all used up."

"Doing what, exactly?" Duffield asked.

The old lady didn't reply, merely stared into the fire, as if an answer might be found there.

Duffield played a hunch.

"You told me earlier about how your father died, how the beast came for him. But that wasn't the end of it, was it? There's more to the story."

"There's always more to stories," Eleanor said. "It's built into their nature. But you don't have time to be listening to mine. And I might not have time to tell it."

"I don't think we can afford not to hear it," Duffield replied. "We need some way of fighting this thing on its own terms. If you know, you need to tell us, before it takes anyone else."

The old lady sighed again.

"There's just one more for it to take…and she's just about ready to go. But if you insist… you'll find a bottle of good sherry and some glasses in the sideboard, Jenny. Fetch us all a drink and gather around… but I'm afraid this isn't a Jackanory story, and there's no happy ever after."

She waited until the drinks were poured then began.

"As I told the lad here earlier, George would have married me after Father passed, no questions asked. But that would have meant either me moving away, or George giving up his job, and neither were scenarios I was willing to give any time to. Besides, the hound was now haunting me, and I had no way of knowing whether it would merely follow me wherever I went. So George stayed in London and I stayed here and over the next few years we drifted apart, even as the hound got closer.

"In those early days I had an obsession by the tail. The hound consumed my every waking moment, whether it was in long hours spent in research in dusty crypts and antiquarian libraries or in nights spent sitting by the cemetery wall watching the thing prowl on Old Tom's Tit, I thought of little else. But all my studies were getting me nowhere. Of course there are many legends, both local and national, of Black Shuck and others like him, across the length and breadth of the country. But I was after something that related to this particular manifestation, looking for meaning for the death of my father and a way to get rid of the brooding thing that haunted both my waking and dreaming lives.

"One night... it was the winter of sixty-three, a particularly bitter one and everything was buried in a blanket of snow... the beast howled and howled, the sound carrying loud in the cold air, and I was close to despair. I turned to my father's old bible for solace and, whether by luck or some divine providence, several sheaves of paper fell out; Father's scribbled, crabbed notes on his own studies into the nature of the beast. I sat in this very chair the whole night, reading them and digesting the import. To cut a long tale short, Father, being a churchman to the core, had approached his problem in a different way to me. Instead of searching directly for the history of the hound, he had instead focussed on the history of the church. His search took him down many historical by-ways and many dead ends but in time he had found the correct thread to pull on, and came up with a timeline and hypothesis which might not be entirely accurate, but feels right to me."

She stopped and coughed. Something sounded broken in her chest and she looked weaker than she had on Duffield's earlier visit, but after some sherry she continued, her voice still strong.

"This village is old. I don't just mean Saxon old, or even Roman old. The foundations in the church crypt are of the same age as the mound we call Old Tom's Tit, and Father's studies were enough to prove that they were Neolithic in nature, perhaps even older. But the 'Tit' isn't a long-barrow. It wasn't built for funereal purposes, was never intended as a resting place at all. The notes Father left showed that it was more in the nature of a prison. Indeed there are indications that, over history, many people have worked to keep it that way. Pre-Roman Celts reinforced the walls with bands of copper, then at a later date iron. Romans poured their strongest concrete, and medieval masons built a stout outer casing over the whole thing. And still the beast within could not be kept quiet.

"Yes, they all knew of the beast, Black Shuck. Father never could find out when it first appeared; he believed it had always been here, somehow tied to this place and that it came straight from Hell. There have been plenty over the centuries who would agree with him, not the least of them being Old Tom himself.

"The main structure of the church and the vicarage in which we sit is Norman, and was built here by Thomas Longbourne, a Saxon in Thrall to the Baron of the area. Thomas by all accounts was somewhat of a scholar of the mystic arts, having travelled extensively with the Baron's entourage in the First Crusade and taking up with other followers of the arts in distant lands. On his return here he set about an attempt to cage the raging beast once and for all.

"There was a great working of high magic. He built the church and reinforced its walls with the blood of his workers, laying down spells and enchantments and once the work was done he called the beast forth to be judged. He bent it to his will and caged it, deep inside the further reinforced mound that carries his name to this day.

"And there it has been, held in place by Thomas' will, and by the wills of the Herdsmen who came in his line after him. I've held him in check these long years, but he's emboldened now that I'm failing."

Duffield, startled, almost spilled his sherry, and that was enough to make Eleanor fall quiet again.

"Herdsman? Why do you use that word?" he asked.

"It's the word my father used," Eleanor replied. "And it's the word used in the ritual."

"Ritual?"

"Yes. The one that Thomas created, the one that has been used by the Herdsmen ever since... the one I have been using these past sixty years to keep the thing at bay. But I'm too old. I haven't the strength. And Shuck knows it."

As if to emphasise the point a loud howl rose up from outside, clear even above the raging of the storm.

"He's close," Eleanor whispered. "I am out of time."

"The ritual? What does it involve?" Duffield asked.

"It's all in the old bible," she said. "It's by my bedside table."

The beast howled again, sounding as if it was outside the window. Eleanor's sherry glass fell from her hands and she coughed again, just once.

By the time Duffield rose from his chair she was slumped in the chair, head on her chest.

He knew she was dead before he reached out to check for a pulse.

The beast howled.

- WIGGO -

Wiggo sat at a table in the bar nursing a pint of beer. The three squaddies were playing brag for matchsticks. Harry, the local, was sleeping again in the corner and Wiggo thought it best to leave him to it. Rain continued to lash, hard, against the windows, and Wiggo's mind kept returning to the flood, wondering how high the waters might reach and whether they were safe, even here close to the high point of the village.

He saw by his watch that it was near midnight, but despite the rigours of the day he no longer felt tired; he was alert, on edge, ready for action and had been ever since the mayhem in the hall.

Mac had been very quiet since they got back to the bar. Wiggo had thought a game of cards might take the lad's mind off things for a wee while, but it didn't seem to be working. The younger private was clearly distracted and, if not actually depressed, not far away from it.

"Could be worse," Wiggo said, deadpan. "It could be raining."

That at least got him a laugh, and Wilkins played his part in keeping the conversation going.

"So, are you glad you didn't get the job, Sarge?"

"I wisnae going to get it anyway, lad," Wiggo replied. "They're not going to give it to a sergeant, and if I get promoted I'll be off the team and out of the game… they don't send staff sergeants out on beastie hunts."

"So what's your plan, Sarge?" Mac asked. "Staff sergeant is a big step up."

"A big step sideways," Wiggo answered. "And too much fucking planning and paperwork for my liking. No. I've decided that I'm happy where I am. Where else would I get paid for sitting in a pub, drinking beer and playing brag? And the lieutenant is doing just fine. I think if we three work together we can make something of him."

Their chat was interrupted by a loud wordless shout from the sleeping Harry, who came up out of sleep with a start and knocked a glass of beer all over the table in front of him. The man's arms thrashed and he stood quickly, almost toppling the table over, before realising where he was.

"Sorry," Harry said sheepishly. "Bad dreams."

"I'm no' surprised lad," Wiggo said. "Come over here, park your arse and have a smoke. The others should be back soon and we'll see what's what."

"They're not going to tell me anything I don't already know," Harry said. "Shuck has got a hard on for me for some reason. It's in my head, in my dreams, and I'm buggered if I know what it wants."

As if in answer a loud howl echoed from somewhere outside.

Wiggo howled back in reply, and even Harry laughed.

"You boys aren't scared of much, are you?"

"Don't let my smooth patter and boyish charm fool you, man," Wiggo replied. "I've been close to shitting myself several times tonight already, and I don't think we're done yet."

"You're probably right, Wiggo," a voice said behind him and Wiggo turned just as the others returned.

"So, a lieutenant, a cop and a barman walk into a bar..." Wiggo said.

Duffield didn't look much in the mood for banter though, and Wiggo let it drop. Silence fell.

"The old lady?" Wiggo asked, and Duffield shook his head.

"She won't be coming."

Harry spoke up.

"Did she say anything?"

"Not much we didn't know already. Although before she passed she spoke of some kind of ritual that might be used to control the beastie. It's supposedly in here."

He fetched out an old cracked leather bible from inside his jacket and showed it around.

"She's dead?" Harry said softly, and Jenny nodded, her breath hitching as she spoke.

"Everybody that didn't leave before the road closed is dead. I think there's just us gathered here left."

"Fuck," Harry said softly.

"Seconded," Wiggo replied.

Wiggo turned to Duffield.

"Options, boss?"

"Precious few, and none of them good ones," Duffield replied. "I'm still keen on hunting this fucker down, especially after what it did in the hall. But running about in the dark is going to get us fucking nowhere."

Harry spoke up quietly.

"What you need is bait. And I think I'm the right worm for that hook."

Wiggo studied the man. The farmer had looked like a long, wet, streak of miserable pish since Wiggo had dragged him out of the water. But something had changed in him just these last few minutes, as if a switch had been flipped. There was a hardness to him that hadn't been evident before, a steel spine that was still straightening. The man looked Wiggo in the eye.

"You've seen it. You know it. It's a hunter, and we're the flock. I'll be the bait, and when it comes, you fellas do your thing, take it down."

"We tried that already," Wiggo said softly. "It didn't work out too well. I think the boss is right; we need brains for this, not guns." He turned to Duffield. "If that auld bugger Seton was here, he'd tell us to read the fucking book, so let's read the fucking book."

Duffield opened up the old bible and four sheaves of vellum fell out. Each sheet was covered in a crabbed script, written in longhand in a dark, almost black ink. The lieutenant began to read, then quickly gave up.

"It's in fucking Latin," he said and dropped the papers on the table. "I don't suppose anybody reads this shite?"

There were blank looks all round the table before Mac spoke quietly.

"I got an O' Level," he said. "I was crap at the oral part but I could read it well enough at the time."

"Well then, lad, here's your chance to upgrade to a Higher," Wiggo said, and handed the papers over to the private, who read to himself quietly while the others looked on. Nobody spoke. Only Mac's lips moved.

"It's some kind of religious chant," the lad said finally.

"No shit, Sherlock?" Wiggo answered. "Is there anything else, any kind of instructions? There's usually instructions."

"Are you some kind of expert then?" Jenny asked.

"Only in blondes, bollocks and bullshit," Wiggo replied. "But usually that's enough to get me through." He turned back to Mac.

"So, no instructions?"

"Just one line. I think it says 'Stand in the old place' although the word doesn't mean 'place' exactly. Could be 'ground'?

"One thing this town's not short of is old places," Duffield said.

"Yep. But there's only a couple long associated with Shuck," Harry said. "It could mean Old Tom's Tit... that's where I first saw it."

"Aye? Good luck with that," Wiggo replied. "If it's no' under water by now it's as good as, as far as getting to it is concerned."

"If not that, it has to be the church," Harry replied.

Duffield spoke up.

"Eleanor told me that's where her father was when he was trying to keep the thing away. In the chapel."

Wiggo looked at Duffield and the lieutenant nodded.

"You've handled this kind of shite before, Wiggo," the officer said. "I'll yield to your better judgement if you think I'm wrong. But the church seems to be our best bet?"

"Aye. That and Mac's O' Level Latin... God help us."

"I think we'll need him on our side," Harry replied. "Although he and I haven't been close for a good long time."

"Probably even longer in my case, lad," Wiggo replied. "But I hear he's a good listener."

"You're still going to need bait."

"And you're still on that hook," Wiggo replied. "Don't worry. We've got your back."

He lifted the glass of beer in front of him and downed it in one gulp.

"Looks like we've got a plan, lads."

- HARRY -

They walked in silence up the hill to the chapel, the officer and youngest soldier in front, Wiggo and the other man bringing up the rear, with Harry, Jenny and Dave sandwiched between them. The wind continued to beat hard against them, driving rain into their faces. The town was dead and empty around them, and Harry was all too aware of what was waiting in the church; the black bags of the dead, waiting to accuse him for his negligence.

That was how he was coming to think of it; the beast had been asking a question of him all the long day, and he'd been spending all his time avoiding it as hard as he could manage. His old life deserved better of him; Wiggo, who'd saved his life, deserved better of him. Plus there was the family tradition to consider, the service to the land... and to the flock.

Are ye a Herdsman yet?

He heard the voice, clear as day inside his head, and decided he'd come to a decision.

"I am," Harry replied, aloud, and Jenny turned to him, eyebrow raised. He waved her away.

"It's nothing. I just realised something."

"Important?"

"To me, yes. To you? We'll soon see."

Once inside the chapel the sound of the wind receded to a distant roar although the rain lashed like tiny whips against the old stained glass windows. A string of high lights flickered and flared, sending shadows dancing around the pews. The black bags weren't as accusing as he'd worried about, although Jenny went pale and quiet at the sight of them. The officer had the soldiers move them all to the far end of the chapel.

Out of sight, not out of mind.

But doing so had cleared an area in front of the altar and pulpit, at the side of the old rough font that was as old as the church itself.

"So, now what?" Jenny asked.

"Time to see if Mac's O' Level is useful for something," Wiggo said.

Duffield handed the sheafs of vellum to the young private.

Mac looked at the papers, then back at Duffield and Wiggo.

"What do I do?"

"Read them," Duffield said.

"Out loud," Wiggo added.

"Fuck," Mac said. "I told you I was shite at this bit."

"Just do your best, lad," Duffield said.

"Aye," Wiggo added. "And if this goes the way things with Seton did, we'll ken soon enough if it's working."

"What about me?" Harry said. "Bait, remember?"

"What do you think you should do?" Wiggo said. "It's you it's got a hard-on for. How do you let it ken you're available?"

"I think that's the easy bit," Harry said softly, and walked away from the others, back to the heavy oak door. He opened it and let the storm hit him full in the face. He shouted out into it.

"I'm here. Where the fuck are you?"

Behind him Mac's voice rose against the wind, halting and nervous at first, but growing in strength and confidence as he found a rhythm in it.

'Dómine, exáudi oratiónem méam. Et clámor meus ad te véniatn nomini et virtute. In nomini et virtute Domini nostri Jesu Christi, eradicare et effugare a Dei Ecclesia, ab animabus ad imaginem Dei conditis ac pretioso divini Agni sanguini redemptis.'

Somewhere out in the night Black Shuck howled.

- DUFFIELD -

As soon as Mac started to declaim in Latin the atmosphere inside the chapel changed. At first Duffield thought it was a change in the wind from outside, but it soon became clear it was internal to the chapel itself, as if the air had become heavy, almost semi-solid, forming a dome of resonance centered directly over where Mac stood by the font. Apart from Harry over by the door, the rest of them were now inside an echoing, thrumming patch of air that started to pulse in time with the words Mac was speaking.

Duffield caught Wiggo's eye. The sergeant winked.

"Same as auld Seton's malarkey. Something's working. Pucker up, boss. I've got a feeling it's going to be a wild ride."

Mac continued to read. He sounded confident now, his voice booming and echoing around the chapel, a priest declaiming to his parishioners.

'Véniat illi láqueus quem ignórat; et cáptio quam abscóndit, apprehéndat eum: et in láqueum cádat in ipsum.'

The air got thicker still. Duffield realised it was warming up around them. The lighting above had taken on a reddish-gold tinge not dissimilar to sunlight.

Another howl sounded outside, much closer than the last.

"The fucker's coming," Wiggo shouted. "Keep at it."

Duffield looked over to the doorway. Harry stood there, arms outstretched as if taunting the thing to come and get him.

Mac kept chanting. It had taken on a sing-song cadence now, words Mac seemed to speak as if he believed them, understood them intimately. The air around them crackled, blue static charges sending forked lightning above their heads in the high rafters.

'Exorcizámos te, ómnis immúnde spíritus, ómnis satánic potéstas, ómnis infernális adversárii, ómnis légio, ómnis congregátio et sécta diabólica, in nómine et virtúte Dómini nóstri Jésu Chrísti.'

Another howl, close enough to raise the hackles at the back of Duffield's neck. There was a movement in the doorway. He looked up to see Harry backing off slowly as a black shadow filled the entrance way. Duffield smelled it now, wet dog, old meat, and felt a cold breeze come in with it, trying to counter the heat that had grown around the font. The lights dimmed overhead, threatened to flicker out. The beast growled, red eyes blazing, and came forward.

Duffield unholstered his weapon, intending to take aim, but felt Wiggo's hand on his arm.

"No, boss. We need smarts on this one, remember? Let Mac do his thing."

The Latin chanting got louder still as the beast took another step into the chapel.

- HARRY -

"Do you have a question for me, fucker?" Harry said as the beast stepped forward.

It looked him in the eye and growled deep in its throat. Its blazing eyes pulsed in time with the rhythm of the Latin chant which echoed all around the chapel as if a choir had raised their voices in unison.

'Váde sátana, invéntor et magíster ómnis falláciae, hóstis humánae salútis. Da lócum Christo, in quo níhil invenísti de opéribus tuis; da lócum Ecclésia Uni, Sanctae, Cathólicae, et Apostólicae, quam Christus ípse acquisívit sánguine suo.'

The beast growled again, and seemed to hesitate just inside the doorway. It was larger than when he'd seen it last, its shoulders almost touching the top of the door frame, its eyes at the same level as his even though its head was lowered. Ropy drool hung from its lower jaw and its stench caught in Harry's throat, threatening to bring on a gag reflex. His every instinct was telling him to run.

But they ran in the Church Hall. And look where that got them.

Harry stood his ground, looked Black Shuck in the eye and did the hardest thing he'd done in his life.

He smiled.

"I asked you a question, fucker," he said. "Do you have anything to say to me?"

The beast continued to stare at him, and Harry suddenly realised why its look felt so familiar; it was exactly like facing down his old ram in the top field when it was trying to show him it was the boss.

Harry's smile turned into a full blown laugh.

"You want to know if I'm a Herdsman? Yes, I'm a fucking Herdsman."

The beast howled. It didn't sound frightening; it sounded like there was some pain in it.

The Latin chanting filled the air; it sounded like all the soldiers plus Jenny and Dave had raised their voices to join in. It sounded like the chapel was full of people.

'Humiliáre sub poténti mánu Dei; contremísce et éffuge, invocáto a nóbis sáncto et terríbili nominé Jésu, quem ínferi trémunt, cui Virtútes caelórum et Potestátes et Dominatiónes subjéctae sunt, quem Chérubim et Séraphim indeféssis vócibus láudant, dicéntes.'

Blue static lightning crackled in the air. The chapel walls and floor pounded in time with the chanting. Harry stamped his feet in unison.

The beast howled, came forward a step, then stopped, as if confused. Harry realised he could see the doorway through it; it was becoming thin, insubstantial.

"Did you hear me, fucker?" Harry shouted. "I'm the fucking Herdsman here now, and you'll do what you're fucking told."

The beast raised its head and howled long and hard.

Harry laughed at it and took a step forward.

"From now on when I tell you to fuck off, you'll fuck off."

The red eyes paled, lost their brilliance. The climax of the Latin chant pounded through the church

'Adjurámus te per Déum vívum, per Déum vérum, per Déum sánctum.'

"Again!" Harry heard Wiggo shout.

'Adjurámus te per Déum vívum, per Déum vérum, per Déum sánctum.'

The beast was almost spectral now, and the eyes, once red, were like black pits.

Harry stepped forward.

The beast took a step back.

The Latin pounded like a vast drumbeat, setting the chapel walls shaking.

'Adjurámus te per Déum vívum, per Déum vérum, per Déum sánctum.'

Harry stepped up, nose to nose with Black Shuck.

"Now fuck off. And don't come back till I say so. I'm the Herdsman here now."

There was a final crack of lightning that momentarily blinded Harry. When he looked again there was nothing at all in the doorway but rain and wind.

The rain seemed to be lessening.

Wiggo came forward as silence fell in the chapel.

"What just happened?" the soldier said.

"It fucked off," Harry replied.

- DUFFIELD -

The final end came the next day. Morning had brought with it a break in the storm. The rain stopped, the wind dropped, the sun came out and the rescue choppers started to arrive; too little, too late.

There was an older man in the first chopper; Duffield recognised George straight away, and took him aside to break the news.

"She's dead?" the old man said, fresh tears in his eyes.

"Yes. But it was quick. She didn't suffer."

"Tell me. But first, I'll need a beer or two."

George got the story over a beer, then insisted he saw Eleanor for the last time. Duffield went with him, but stayed in the adjoining room as the old couple had a final goodbye. The old man had more tears in his eyes as they left, and something in his hand.

"It's a letter," he said. "She had it up her sleeve. It's addressed to the farmer, Harry."

They found Harry with Wiggo and the others in the pub. George handed him the letter. Harry opened it, read it, then read it aloud. This time it was him who had tears in his eyes.

Dear Harry,

I think I've always known who would be next. My will leaves everything to you. My solicitor should be in touch when word of my passing reaches him.

You're the Herdsman now. Take care of my... your... flock.

Yours in companionship forever
Eleanor Wilkes
Herdswoman.

CHECK OUT OTHER GREAT CRYPTID NOVELS

BIGFOOT WAR
by Eric S. Brown

Now a feature film from Origin Releasing. For the first time ever, all three core books of the Bigfoot War series have been collected into a single tome of Sasquatch Apocalypse horror. Remastered and reedited this book chronicles the original war between man and beast from the initial battles in Babblecreek through the apocalypse to the wastelands of a dark future world where Sasquatch reigns supreme and mankind struggles to survive. If you think you've experienced Bigfoot Horror before, think again. Bigfoot War sets the bar for the genre and will leave you praying that you never have to go into the woods again.

CRYPTID ZOO
by Gerry Griffiths

As a child, rare and unusual animals, especially cryptid creatures, always fascinated Carter Wilde.

Now that he's an eccentric billionaire and runs the largest conglomerate of high-tech companies all over the world, he can finally achieve his wildest dream of building the most incredible theme park ever conceived on the planet...CRYPTID ZOO.

Even though there have been apparent problems with the project, Wilde still decides to send some of his marketing employees and their families on a forced vacation to assess the theme park in preparation for Opening Day.

Nick Wells and his family are some of those chosen and are about to embark on what will become the most terror-filled weekend of their lives—praying they survive.

STEP RIGHT UP AND GET YOUR FREE PASS...

TO CRYPTID ZOO

CHECK OUT OTHER GREAT CRYPTID NOVELS

SWAMP MONSTER MASSACRE
by Hunter Shea

The swamp belongs to them. Humans are only prey. Deep in the overgrown swamps of Florida, where humans rarely dare to enter, lives a race of creatures long thought to be only the stuff of legend. They walk upright but are stronger, taller and more brutal than any man. And when a small boat of tourists, held captive by a fleeing criminal, accidentally kills one of the swamp dwellers' young, the creatures are filled with a terrifyingly human emotion—a merciless lust for vengeance that will paint the trees red with blood.

TERROR MOUNTAIN
by Gerry Griffiths

When Marcus Pike inherits his grandfather's farm and moves his family out to the country, he has no idea there's an unholy terror running rampant about the mountainous farming community. Sheriff Avery Anderson has seen the heinous carnage and the mutilated bodies. He's also seen the giant footprints left in the snow—Bigfoot tracks. Meanwhile, Cole Wagner, and his wife, Kate, are prospecting their gold claim farther up the valley, unaware of the impending dangers lurking in the woods as an early winter storm sets in. Soon the snowy countryside will run red with blood on TERROR MOUNTAIN.

CHECK OUT OTHER GREAT BIGFOOT NOVELS

THE BEASTS OF STONECLAD MOUNTAIN
by **Gerry Griffiths**

Clay Morgan is overjoyed when he is offered a place to live in a remote wilderness at the base of a notorious mountain. Locals say there are Bigfoot living high up in the dense mountainous forest. Clay is skeptic at first and thinks it's nothing more than tall tales.

But soon Clay becomes a believer when giant creatures invade his new home and snatch his baby boy, Casey.

Now, Clay and his wife, Mia, must rescue their son with the help of Clay's uncle and his dog, a journey up the foreboding mountain that will take them into an unimaginable world...straight into hell!

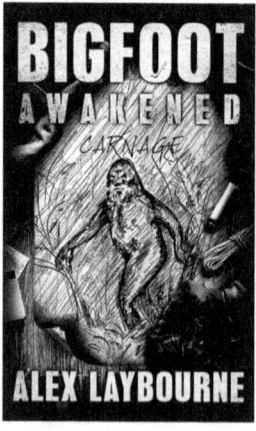

BIGFOOT AWAKENED
by **Alex Laybourne**

A weekend away with friends was supposed to be fun. One last chance for Jamie to blow off some steam before she leaves for college, but when the group make a wrong turn, fun is the last thing they find.

From the moment they pass through a small rural town they are being hunted by whatever abominations live in the woods.

Yet, as the beasts attack and the truth is revealed, they learn that despite everything, man still remains the most terrifying evil of them all.

www.ingramcontent.com/pod-product-compliance
Lightning Source LLC
Chambersburg PA
CBHW061249170626
46809CB00007B/2920